COZUMEL ESCAPE

Destination Billionaire Romance

CAMI CHECKETTS

Birch River Publishing

COPYRIGHT

INTRODUCTION

I was one of those kids that always wanted to eat dessert first, but it was never allowed. Now that I'm an adult, I often do! The Destination Billionaire Romance Series reminds me of dessert because it allows you to get right to the good stuff—exotic locations, billionaires, and plenty of passionate kisses that take your breath away. I love the freshness of this series and how the characters are as unique as their locations. Like a smooth, creamy, delectable dessert, I savor each tender love story and eagerly await the next one. So, sit back and relax. Fall in love again and again. Because, let's face it, everyone needs a little dessert. And this time, you can eat it first!

Jennifer Youngblood, author of *Love on the Rocks* (Hawaii Billionaire Romance Series)

FREE BILLIONAIRE BRIDE PACT ROMANCE

Sign up for Cami's newsletter and receive a free ebook copy of *The Feisty One: A Billionaire Bride Pact Romance* here.

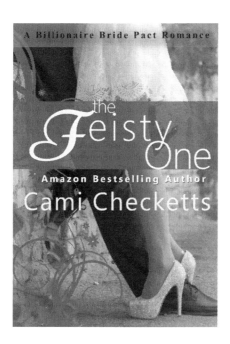

To my parents. Thank you for your unconditional love.

CHAPTER ONE

Brooks Hoffman whistled as he walked along the touristy marketplace of Cozumel. It was a beautiful eighty degrees with a slight breeze coming off the ocean, and since there wasn't a cruise ship in town today, the market was a bit quieter than usual. That meant fewer women, but there were sacrifices he was willing to make for a peaceful shopping trip before Christmas.

He'd already found toys for Zack and Maddie's three children, but he wanted to find something pretty for Maddie, and he had no clue what to buy Zack. His closest friend was taking his family to New York for the holidays to be with his parents. If Brooks wanted to give them presents, he'd have to be ready when he went to visit them on their island for Thanksgiving weekend.

A gorgeous, pint-sized blonde breezed in front of him, tossing him an intriguing smile, her blue eyes sparkling. She ducked into a women's clothing shop before he could turn on the charm.

What was that little dream doing on his island? No cruise ships in port meant she was staying for a week or beyond. Dare he hope she was here for longer than a week? He tsked at himself. He'd never dated any woman longer than a week, so what did it matter? His grin grew.

This one was intriguing enough that it might take longer than a week to tire of her.

He followed her light scent into the women's shop. Apparently, this was the place Maddie would receive her Christmas present from this year.

"Can I help you?" the young attendant called out while folding a cobalt-blue shirt. She glanced up and smiled at him. "Ah. Señor Hoffman. So good to see you, sir."

"You as well." Most of the island knew Brooks by name. He hired a lot of locals, and they'd become his close friends. What could he say? This was his kingdom. Of course they revered him.

He glanced around for the woman. She was in the back, sifting through long dresses on a rack. He sidled his way up to her, bent down, and murmured, "The blue would match your eyes beautifully."

She jumped and took a swing at him.

Brooks stepped back quickly to avoid getting smacked by the woman. She was so small he could bench-press her without raising his heart rate, but her punch had been quick and sure.

"Oh, sorry!" Her cheeks reddened. *How intriguing, a woman that blushed easily.* "I didn't hear you approach, and all of a sudden you're, like, whispering in my ear."

Brooks arched an eyebrow. He liked the way she talked—blunt, and with a Southern accent that could drive a man to buy unnecessary jewelry.

"How in the world did you sneak up on me? You're stinking huge!"

"Training." He was never going to elaborate. "So, South Carolina? Maybe Georgia?"

"Alabama."

"Ah. I like it. Here for a week, or can I persuade you to stay longer?" He winked, and she blushed again. *Ah, innocence.* It could never be bested in his opinion.

"I live here." Her lips turned down and she brushed by him. "If you'll excuse me."

Brooks reached out and gently gripped her arm. She glared down at his fingers, then up at him. How could a woman this interesting live here, on his island, and he not know about it?

"I don't know if I can excuse you." He took his voice to the depth he knew drove women crazy. "I haven't seen eyes that brilliantly blue in years and find myself quite drawn to you. Dinner tonight?"

"No, but thanks all the same for the invite," she said, with just the right amount of sauce in her voice, like Southern barbecue—sweet and tangy.

"You can thank me later," he murmured.

Those blue eyes snapped up at him, and her pretty pink lips puckered as if she'd licked the salt off of a margarita. Hmm. Salt, margaritas, and her lips. He liked it.

She tugged her arm back, and he released her because he was a gentleman first and foremost. As a child, he'd seen too many men take advantage of women. That would never be him.

She speed walked to the front of the shop. Luckily for both of them, he was quick as a panther. "At least tell me where you're staying. If you're lucky enough, I could convince you to have drinks with me."

She whirled, and her eyes went up his body, down, and up again. Brooks flexed his arms slightly, certain she would like what she saw. A man doesn't spend hours in the gym every day for his health.

Tilting her head to the side, she let that luscious blonde hair spill over her toned and tanned shoulder. He looked forward to an opportunity to pick her up and kiss her until she begged for more. Ah. His life was good.

"I don't drink."

"Oh? Dinner then." He dusted his hands off. It was settled. "When and where shall I pick you up?"

She took a step closer to him, and he couldn't hide a smile of triumph. She'd come around quickly. They always did.

"You can come have dinner with us. I believe our cook is whipping up somethin' special tonight." That accent was being applied thick as frosting. "Tortillas and beans."

Tortillas and beans? Was she kidding? Any child on the island could make tortillas and beans. "Hmm? Yes, while that does sound appetizing ..." She was appetizing, but her dinner offer definitely was not. Yet, it was an opportunity to spend time with her. Sometimes good food had to be sacrificed to woo said lady. "Where is this dinner to be held?"

"Bethel Orphanage. You might've heard of it, just a half mile inland from here." She whirled and stomped from the store.

Brooks' jaw unhinged. Sheer terror rushed through him at the idea of setting foot in the building. The orphanage? He donated vast amounts of money to that orphanage, but had never made it past the wooden front door. The memories of hunger and pain would crash around him, and someone might find out that the mighty Brooks Hoffman was simply a scared little boy who had buried his past rather than deal with it.

"Are you going to go?" The smooth-skinned shopkeeper was by his side.

Brooks pasted his confident smile back on. "Ah, no. I've had enough tortillas and beans to last me a lifetime." He threw his shoulders back and strutted out of the shop before she asked any more questions.

CHAPTER TWO

D aniel sighed, giving the exhale all the attitude a pre-teen should have, and bared his teeth.

"You flossed, too?" Sydnee wasn't fooled by his fake grumpiness. He was a great young man and loved her as much as he loved and watched out for all the younger children.

The twelve-year-old nodded, but Sydnee waited. The director liked to utilize Sydnee to teach the children English. Sydnee figured it was because she struggled with Spanish with her Southern accent, always distorting what she meant to say. She'd overheard her college Spanish teacher telling his assistant that Sydnee might as well have been speaking with a rag stuffed in her mouth, and that no local would ever understand her.

She reassured herself that English was a great skill for the kids to acquire. It opened up opportunities for the older children with work, school, and chances to leave the island that they wouldn't have other-wise. Daniel spoke extremely well, but she still encouraged him to use English as much as possible.

"Yes, ma'am, Mees Sydnee."

"Good job, bud." Sydnee loved how the children said *Mees* instead of *Miss*. Adorable. She gave Daniel a side hug and ushered him toward the boy's room. "Go say your prayers and I'll come sing to the little ones in a few minutes."

Daniel smiled, ducking his head in embarrassment at the hug, but she knew he needed the physical touch.

"You're almost as tall as me," she exclaimed.

His smile grew. "Not hard to do."

"Ha. Go!"

Daniel gave her a quick squeeze, then darted down the hallway. Sydnee glanced around at an empty bathroom. The sink was covered in toothpaste, but at least all the boys had clean teeth tonight. Thank heavens the cleaning crew would be by in the morning. Sydnee and Rosmerta expected the children to pitch in on day-to-day pickup and wipe-up, but the deep cleaning done by some local ladies each week was help they needed and appreciated.

She wondered if Rosmerta had had as good of luck with the girls' teeth. They rotated assignments putting the boys and the girls to bed each night. Sydnee loved them all and just wished there was more of her to go around. They needed more hugs, more love, and more training. They especially needed male influences in their lives. The orphanage was extremely well funded from a private donor on the island. Without that generous funding, they wouldn't be able to run the orphanage, let alone afford cooks and maid service. And without that extra help around the house, Sydnee, Camila, and Rosmerta wouldn't have nearly as much time to hug and teach.

Sydnee had asked the director, Camila, many times if she couldn't meet and thank the man. Camila always insisted that the man was adamant about remaining anonymous, or he would pull his funding. What an odd duck. But the three women were grateful for him nonetheless. Without his money there wouldn't be a Bethel Orphanage, and Sydnee couldn't imagine where these children would be then.

She could hear the girls still brushing and laughing with Rosmerta in their bathroom. The boys were a lot quicker to get ready at night. It was awkward without a man around to help the boys with their toiletries. Even though they could offer a decent wage, they hadn't found a man they were comfortable with around the children. Human trafficking was a huge problem with orphanages, and they'd heard of several terrifying stories throughout Mexico. So for the time being, it was just three women and eighteen children ranging from six months to twelve years old.

The orphanage was tucked half a mile inland, so they didn't usually see tourists and were hopefully off the traffickers' radar. The privacy was nice, especially away from overconfident men like that muscle-bound guy from the clothing store today. Sydnee couldn't help but smile as she thought of the interaction. He may have been a jerk, but he was a handsome, witty jerk.

Sydnee walked down the hallway to check on the nursery before she went to sing the boys to sleep. Camila had thought it was odd to spend time singing children to sleep when Sydnee first came to volunteer three years ago during summer break from New York University. When Sydnee returned to the island full time after college graduation fifteen months ago, Camila admitted she'd implemented singing every night. The children went to sleep easier, slept through the night better, and seemed to wake up happier.

Voices drifted from Camila's open office door.

"Gracias, Mr. Hoffman, gracias. It is such a pleasure to finally meet you and be able to thank you. We would have to close our doors without your funding."

"Glad to help." The deep bass seemed familiar to Sydnee. Curiosity to see their donor and to figure out how she knew that voice had her creeping closer to the private conversation like a fox stalking the chicken coop.

"I just can't express enough how grateful we are for your funding. It has saved us and made it possible to help and love the children rather than spend our days trying to drum up money to provide the basics."

"Good, good." The man sounded uncomfortable. Who wouldn't be under that kind of praise? "I was hoping ..." He paused and cleared his throat. "Do you have a beautiful little blonde working for you now?"

Sydnee flattened her back against the wall. The guy from the dress shop! No way. *He* was their benefactor? Her cheeks flushed just thinking about his handsome face with the strong cheekbones, square jaw, piercing dark eyes, and the most beautiful lips she'd ever seen on a man. His hair had been dark and longer on top, with just a little bit of curl to it. His body was ... well, it was obvious he worked out ... a lot. The biceps and triceps revealed by his short-sleeved shirt had left her mouth dry. He'd been far too flirtatious, so she'd run as fast as possible. She had no problem with men, but she didn't like empty flirtations. At least, she hadn't until today, when the man in her boss's office had brought all kinds of color and imagination to her life. She'd daydreamed about him throughout the rest of the day but was certain she wouldn't see him again. She'd been here for over a year and rarely had time to leave the orphanage or meet anyone beyond these walls.

"Well," Camila said, her voice cautious, "Sydnee is petite and has long, blonde hair."

"Does she now? Can I please speak with this Sydnee?"

"Of course. Anything you want, Mr. Hoffman."

Anything he wanted indeed. Camila, and really all of them, owed this Mr. Hoffman the roof over their heads, the food on their table, and every opportunity they had for the children. If he wanted Sydnee to do the rumba for him, Camila would demand she do it.

Sydnee pushed away from the wall and ran for the nursery. She'd hide out in there. There was no way she could face that man again, especially now that she knew who he really was. She was grateful to him, but not sure she was prepared to do anything he wanted. She'd dated a lot of great guys in high school and college, spending most of her free time with her semi-boyfriend, Jace, but she'd never dated someone with the looks and charisma that their benefactor possessed. He was ... overwhelming.

Since she'd been on the island, she'd hardly gone on a date. There had been a few men who'd expressed interest, but she was too busy with the children. They had to come first in somebody's life, and thankfully Camila and Rosmerta were as dedicated as Sydnee was to teaching and loving them.

She shut the nursery door softly behind her. There were only three cribs in use now, as Mateo had turned three and insisted he be in with the big boys.

Her heart calmed immediately as she listened to the soft breathing of the babies. Brushing her fingers over Tomás's wispy curls, she couldn't resist leaning down and kissing his soft cheek. He smelled as yummy as any six-month-old baby should, and she felt another surge of gratitude for Mr. Hoffman. He may have been an overconfident flirt, but the man spoiled them all financially. She knew most orphanages couldn't afford to keep their children clean, well fed, and well dressed like Bethel could.

Staying in the nursery longer than she should have, she tucked blankets around each little one and said a prayer over them. She slipped out the door and ran into a solid body of muscle.

"Oomph!" Sydnee bounced back against the wall.

Mr. Hoffman's brow furrowed as he reached out to steady her with his warm hands.

Sydnee felt the connection down to her toes. When he'd touched her earlier today, it had been the most pleasant current, and here it was again. No. She couldn't be sucked in by this schmoozer. Her daddy would have her hide if she let herself fall for a worldly man instead of a good Southern boy like Jace. Yet Jace was an international businessman now who sadly had never sent her nerves tingling with a simple touch and glance.

"Are you okay, beautiful girl?" Mr. Hoffman murmured.

"Yes, I'm fine." The empty compliment brought her up straight. He was obviously a generous man who liked to donate his money and was very free with his words as well. She steeled her spine. *Be leery. Be smart.*

"I had hoped to see you again," he murmured, his eyes tracing over her face like a caress.

This man could suck her in faster than quicksand. She must be strong.

"So you finally set your big ole boots on our hallowed soil?" She placed a hand on her hip and glared at him. "We've all been hoping to meet you and thank you for years. But you get snubbed by a woman for a dinner invite and suddenly you're willing to grace the orphanage you self-fund with your presence?" She laid the drawl on thick. She'd gone to NYU for four years before graduating and moving here. Most of the time her accent was subtle, but when she got fired up, her claws came out and she used all the snotty tactics she remembered from the cat-fighting women back home.

He took a step back, his chin tucking in like she'd struck him or something. "You know who I am?"

"Yessiree, Mr. Hoffman. I know who you are." She blinked, forced her hands to unclench, and softened her tone. "And we're all mighty grateful to you for the generosity."

Mr. Hoffman took a step forward again. "Grateful enough to have dinner with me tomorrow?"

Sydnee was paralyzed by the way his dark eyes focused in on her like she was the most beautiful woman in the world and the only woman he'd ever look at that way. That was desperate thinking, and she wasn't a desperate woman. She shook her head and glanced down the hallway.

Camila was leaning out of her office and gesturing wildly to her. "Yes, yes," she mouthed.

Sydnee rolled her eyes. She knew that would be the reaction she'd get from her boss. Sydnee would do anything for the children, but maybe not ... anything. How far was Mr. Hoffman going to push? He had to realize the henhouse he was trapping her in if she refused. Camila would peck away at her until her head was a nubbin. Their entire operation and the children's safety, happiness, and security depended on this much-too-intriguing man. How could she possibly refuse a dinner invite from him?

"I would love to, Mr. Hoffman." Sydnee sighed and bit at her lip.

His perfectly formed fingers lifted; then he cautiously reached out and caressed her jaw. Sydnee found herself tilting toward his touch. He leaned close and whispered, "It's Brooks, my love."

Sydnee's gaze jumped to his. How dare he call her *his love* and give her these searing looks. He assumed way too much from a simple dinner date. He was nothing but a player, and no matter how they all depended on him, she was not a plaything here for his enjoyment.

"Where and when would you like me to meet you tomorrow, *Mr. Hoffman*?"

His fingers dropped from her face. He smiled the indulgent smile she reserved for a small child. "I'll send a car around seven, *Sydnee*."

She flinched at the intimate way he said her name. Whatever happened, she would preserve her innocence. She wanted him out of here, now, and suddenly she had an idea she thought might knock some swagger out of him.

"Would you like to come visit with some of the children?" She batted her eyelashes while issuing the challenge. "It's bedtime, and they'd just love to hear a song or story from their noble benefactor."

All the arrogance dropped from his face, and he backed away like she'd tried to tase him. "Oh, um, no. Thank you for the offer, love, but I'm very ... busy."

He gave her a cheeky grin that only had half of the power of his earlier smiles, thank heavens, then spun on his leather boot, which probably cost more than their food budget, and almost ran from the building.

"What was all that about?" Rosmerta asked from behind her.

"Rich American wants to donate all the money we need, but isn't willing to get his hands sticky. When are we ever going to find a man who wants to be part of the children's lives?" Sydnee wanted him to interact with everyone in the building, herself included. He may have been a filthy rich, philandering man, but she was still drawn to him. She knew the children, particularly Daniel, the oldest and most in need of a father figure in his life, would love simply being around a strong male, especially one with a smile and sense of humor like Brooks—or rather, Mr. Hoffman—seemed to have.

"Oh, well." Rosmerta watched him go. "At least the view of him running away is nice."

Sydnee giggled, and then had to cover her hand with her mouth. "I don't know what you're talking about."

"Liar. I saw you checking him out."

"There was a lot of him to check out."

Rosmerta sucked in a breath and licked her lips. "Yes, there was."

CHAPTER THREE

Brooks drummed his fingers against his Armani suit pants and closed his eyes in a brief prayer. He wanted tonight to go well. This little Sydnee doll did not seem to be receptive to his immense charm like ninety-nine percent of the women in the world. He was afraid the only reason she'd agreed was the pressure from her boss mouthing "yes" down the hallway. He hoped he was wrong, but she'd almost acted like she didn't trust him, as if he would pull his financial support if their date wasn't up to par. He smiled to himself. He'd never had to coerce a woman to fall for his magnetism. They usually took one look at his face and body, he'd smile and stare into their eyes, and bam, they'd happily have his babies if he asked. He never asked. If he could get Sydnee to swoon for him, he might be asking.

"Ha!" he laughed out loud.

"Boss?" José turned slightly in the front seat of the Hummer.

"Nothing, my friend. It's all good." He smiled. He'd never ask any woman to have his babies, as he was a good Christian boy first and foremost, so to have babies meant a ring on someone's finger. He was never going to settle down. He'd bought plenty of jewelry for beautiful women, but drew the line at rings. Rings meant scary words like *commitment* and *playtime over for Brooks*. No rings, ever.

They pulled up to the Bethel Orphanage, and Brooks felt a surge of pride. Anything the director, Camila, asked for, he gave the money or had someone see to the details. The entire property was well kept. Along the back side of the large home was a grassy area and lots of commercial play equipment, slides, swings, and forts to climb, hide, and pretend in. He paid for maintenance crews to come regularly, including a weekly cleaning crew, and everything was in good working order. It was miles above what he'd had before Mr. Hoffman adopted him.

His lips pursed. Had Sydnee been teasing him about having only tortillas and beans for dinner? He'd check into that. They should have money for the food they wanted and a good variety for the children. Camila said they had eleven boys and seven girls in the house right now. Those children needed meat, veggies, and fruit. The boys especially needed meat if they were going to grow big and strong like him.

He puffed out his chest, more than proud of his physique and all that he'd accomplished with the money his adoptive father had bestowed when he passed away ten years ago.

The car rolled to a stop, and Brooks jumped out before José could get his door. His thoughts returned to Sydnee and his hope for some lip action after tonight's dinner. How he loved beautiful women. With any luck, he'd convince this one that he was a man worth loving on.

The front door swung open and Sydnee rushed out, shutting it quickly behind her like the hounds of Hades were on her heels. She wore a flowing white dress that drew attention to her tan shoulders and nicely formed calf muscles. Her hair draped down her back in long waves. A bold, jade necklace accented her neckline. Her blue eyes looked brighter with eye makeup highlighting them, and her naturally pink lips were a dramatic red. He liked it. Oh yes, he did. She'd made an effort to be even more attractive. For him. This night was going to go so well.

Sydnee strode past him with her head held high and her shoulders back, as if she were marching to her inevitable execution, and grabbed on to the door handle of the sport utility vehicle. José was there to swing it open. She slid inside without saying a word to either of them.

Brooks swallowed the compliment he'd been ready to bestow. Maybe tonight wasn't going to go so well, after all.

José glanced his way with a question in his eyes. Brooks shrugged and walked around the Hummer. José opened his door. "Thank you, mi amigo," Brooks murmured.

He reclined into the soft leather of the backseat and turned toward Sydnee, giving her his award-winning smile. "You look extremely beautiful tonight."

She glared at him. "Let's get something straight. I am not one of your little hoochie mamas. I can't be bought. And the only reason I'm coming to dinner is so Camila can get her panties out of a wad!"

Brooks reared back in surprise. "What would lead you to believe that I have *hoochie mamas?*" He wasn't quite sure if she knew what that meant to most people.

Sydnee rolled her eyes. "I'm not dumb. You're a buff, good-looking, wealthy flirt. You have women lining up to lick your toe lint, so don't act like I'm something special when I'm not."

Brooks had never been more insulted, even though she'd given him some backhanded compliments. For some reason, it upset him that she didn't think *she* was something special. He'd spent most of his life knowing he wasn't. "I do *not* have toe lint," he said.

Sydnee actually smiled at that, but her lips turned down quickly. "Let's make a deal, Mr. Hoffman."

He held up a hand. "First part of the deal is you call me Brooks."

"Okay, Brooks," she spat out between her teeth.

"Say it nicely." He smiled at her, enjoying their sparring even though the hope of a kiss was buried beneath pounds of her obvious resentment of having to go out with him.

She swallowed, and her eyes roved over his face. He successfully hid a smirk at her obvious appreciation. She wanted him. She just didn't know it yet.

He leaned in, maintaining eye contact. Her chest rose and fell quickly. Her eyes dipped down to his lips, then back up. Every woman loved his lips. He could hear Sydnee's shortened breaths and smell something delectable. She reminded him of sweet lemon candy. Would she taste just as good? Brooks really enjoyed the effect he was having on her. Oh yes, women made his life so enjoyable.

"Brooks," she murmured.

He grinned and wrapped an arm around the back of her seat. "Thank you." He dipped his head to within inches of hers. His lips hovered over hers, and that hint of citrus was infused with peppermint. Yes, she was going to taste delicious.

Her hands rested on his chest. Slowly, she rubbed them across his pectoral muscles. He knew from years of experience that women died over his well-developed pecs. Her touch started a low burn in his stomach. He needed to slow down the moment before the kiss, but he felt like a teenager on his first date. He could hardly stand the anticipation. He cupped her cheek with his palm. She was soft and smelled great, and he wanted to devour her right here and now. Forget that his friend José was sitting in the front seat and the car wasn't moving.

"Brooks?" she whispered again, and he loved the sound of her saying his name.

"Hmm?" He lowered his other hand along her back, pulling her closer to him.

Her hands hardened into fists, and she pushed him back.

Brooks straightened in surprise. His hand fell away from her face. Had he just been rejected?

"The deal is, I have dinner with you, and you keep funding the orphanage. Don't you think for one second that you can extort me into dating you. If you pull your funding, you can bet your muscled chest that I'll find a way to take care of those children. I would die for them, but I wouldn't kiss *you* for a million bucks."

Brooks felt like he'd just been stabbed with a knife. His sweet beauty had a bite to her that he didn't know if he liked or not.

"Thank you for telling me how you really feel," he shot back at her.

"You have no idea," she said, but her voice sounded tired instead of feisty.

Straightening his shoulders and tilting his head to the side, he bestowed his irresistible signature grin on her. He never backed down from a challenge. Little did she know that he was just getting started.

Sydnee could hardly catch a breath as they coasted to a stop at the end of a long, tree-lined drive. The driver got her door, and Brooks rushed around to her side of the car and was waiting there with his arm extended.

She studied him, not sure if she could handle even the simple touch of her hand through his arm. What kind of man didn't get offended by being put in his place? She'd been sure he would take her back to the orphanage and inform Camila that he was done providing for them. But no, he thanked her and then gave her that grin. Good heavens. How many women had fallen to the ground groveling under the power of that grin, the smoldering look in those dark eyes? He was good, she'd give him that.

She'd almost kissed him. She'd wanted to scream for joy at how amazing his touch had felt and cry at the loss of it. Thankfully, she'd found some self-control she didn't know she possessed and pushed him away. Her words were too harsh. If he hadn't been such an overconfident playboy, she would've been very interested in dating him. She liked the way he talked, the way he moved, and especially the way he looked at her. No. She was smarter than falling for some wealthy guy who only wanted a one-night stand. At least, she hoped she was.

She turned and stared at the massive house. Mangrove trees lined the road leading up to the stucco mansion, but she could see the beach and palm trees stretching out behind the house.

Brooks escorted her up the wide front stairs. It was a sprawling two-story affair that fit well with the local culture.

"How long have you lived here?" Sydnee asked.

"Five years. You like my little hacienda?"

"It'll do," Sydnee said flippantly, stifling a laugh at the obvious disappointment in his eyes.

They walked through nine-foot doors into a cavernous entryway with a sweeping staircase on the left.

"Before I met you, I felt bad that you gave so much to the orphanage. Now I can see it's like toilet paper to you."

"Toilet paper?" Brooks looked down at her with a question in his eyes.

"You could use money like toilet paper and flush it away."

"I like Charmin better, though."

Sydnee laughed. She couldn't help it. Brooks gave her that grin that made her want to melt into a puddle at his feet. She straightened her spine and wiped the smile from her face. *Stay strong. He makes every woman laugh and want to melt. You're not falling for that.*

Brooks quirked an eyebrow, but didn't comment on her sudden lack of mirth. He escorted her through the entry into a large great room, taking the time to thank the small cook profusely for all her hard work.

"This is my new friend, Sydnee," Brooks said, presenting her. "Valentina," he said to Sydnee, "the best cook and little momma on the island."

Valentina laughed and took Sydnee's hand. "Is very nice to meet you, Mees Sydnee," she said with a heavy accent.

"You too." Sydnee found she meant it. The woman seemed like a little momma who would take care of everyone around her. Sydnee had to admit that the way Brooks treated his staff was impressive. Like they were his friends. Probably just trying to trick Sydnee into thinking he was a good guy. She shook her head. He had to be a good guy. Nobody self-funded an orphanage without having some pretty impressive charity on the inside. She glanced at him. His body was big enough to hold lots of charity. Maybe she'd been too harsh on him.

"I hope you enjoy dinner," Valentina said, then turned back to the stove.

"I'm sure I will," Sydnee returned. "Thank you."

Brooks wrapped an arm around her waist and escorted her past the kitchen and dining area to a back patio that overlooked the beach and ocean beyond. The sun dipped low on the horizon, the palm trees swayed, waves lapped against the beach, and you couldn't have picked a more romantic setting.

"You're sure you'll enjoy dinner?" Brooks said, his breath tickling her ear.

Sydnee jumped and whirled on him. "Stop with the suave act. Treat me the way you'd treat Valentina."

His eyebrows rose. "My little momma?" Brooks trailed a hand through her hair and rested it on her shoulder.

She trembled under his touch, and her body swayed closer to his without her permission.

"I don't think my sixty-year-old friend would appreciate me wanting to touch her soft skin or kiss her cherry-red lips." His finger brushed Sydnee's lips, and they parted under his touch. Sydnee's breath was coming in quick pants. She studied his firm lips, intrigued by the way his top lip bowed and his bottom lip was slightly fuller. Those lips were almost too pretty for a man. Almost. She suddenly wanted with everything in her to see what they would taste like.

Sydnee forced herself to step back, but the smirk on Brooks's face showed he knew how much he affected her. When her breathing was under control, she muttered, "Well, this twenty-three-year-old social worker doesn't appreciate wanting to touch you. I mean ..." She blew out all her breath. This was not going well. Brushing past him, she walked down toward the ocean. She needed a break.

Of course Brooks followed her. She stopped and folded her arms across her chest, watching the waves softly rolling onto the shore. She loved the peaceful Caribbean waters.

"Are you okay?" Brooks asked from behind her.

Sydnee shook her head, really not sure. Why had she agreed to this dinner? This man was too much for her. She wanted to believe that since she hadn't been around an attractive man for so long, her body responded like this just because of her lack of male companionship. Yet she'd gone home for a few weeks this summer and spent time with her large family and her friends. Jace had taken her on some fun dates. He was a great guy, extremely good-looking, and she'd had fun seeing him. She had even let him give her a quick kiss goodbye, but she felt nothing like she was feeling right now.

"I really can't do this," she finally managed.

Brooks walked around in front of her so she had to face him. "Do what, pretty girl?"

"Exactly! I don't want you giving me compliments. I don't want you kissing me." She blushed, and he grinned. "And I don't want you trying to get into my pants!"

"Whoa." Brooks took a step back and lifted his hands. "The compliments come because I think you are a work of art. The kissing will come because you want me whether you'll admit it or not." He winked, and she couldn't have looked away from the sparkle in his dark eyes if she'd tried. "But I would not begin to try to get into your pants." He pulled a cross out from under his shirt. "Christian."

"What?" Sydnee grabbed at his silver cross and stared up at him. "You're a Christian?"

He nodded.

"When?" He didn't want to get into her pants? He wasn't a player—well, at least not to that extreme. He needed to get talking and explaining.

"When?" he asked.

"When did you convert? Have you always been filthy rich? Why the orphanage when you don't want to interact with the children? Why do you live on Cozumel when you're obviously American?" The sight of the cross had opened a gate in her wall. A wall she'd thought was pretty well built—except for this one admission that let Brooks slip through. She'd been raised strong in the faith, and the devoted Christian men she knew were the type of men she could trust.

"Maybe one question at a time." He arched an eyebrow. "Simple explanation—I wouldn't be giving this much to the orphanage if I didn't believe in a higher power."

She nodded and saw him in a whole new light. "The Lord directed you to help?"

"He gave me all of this." He gestured to the property behind them. "The least I can do is help others."

"You're not what I expected, Brooks Hoffman."

Brooks gave her a compassionate smile. "Somebody's changing their opinion of the big guy."

"Maybe." She startled as she realized how quickly she'd let her guard down. Anyone could claim to be a Christian. "We'll see."

He pointed back toward the patio. "How about we eat dinner and get to know each other a little bit?"

"Okay." She walked by his side through the sand and up the patio steps. "But I'm still not giving you a kiss tonight." She blushed. Why did she have to bring the conversation back to that?

His eyebrows arched up. "We'll see."

CHAPTER FOUR

B rooks popped a bite of coconut shrimp in his mouth and savored the zest of the sauce and the crunch of the flavorful shrimp. The little lady had warmed considerably since she'd seen the cross around his neck. Interesting. Why hadn't he thought of that before?

Shame scratched at his conscience. Mr. Hoffman had taught him better than that. The cross was a symbol of his love for the Savior, and he used it to remind himself of who and what he needed to be, not to get the praise of man or woman.

The sun had long set, but soft tiki lights lit the beach area, and candles were scattered around the patio. They talked about the children at the orphanage, and he shared the different connections he had with his friends who worked for him. He also talked a little bit about Zack and Maddie and their three children, two of whom were adopted from Belize and one who was Zack's niece.

Luckily, he avoided much of his back story by simply telling her he'd been raised in Fresno, and a rich benefactor had started him in the world of hard money loans where he'd increased his fortune. He'd never told a date about his lack of a childhood, his adoptive father, his conversion, or the inheritance. Though, he was tempted to share more with Sydnee than was smart when she looked at him with those big blue eyes.

"Do you miss your family?" he asked, more because it was the right follow-up question after she'd talked about her huge extended family than because he wanted to hear about an intact family unit. Maybe some with his background would be curious how a whole family interacted. He was not.

Sydnee set her fork down and stared out at the dark ocean. "I do. My brothers and sisters are great, and my parents worked hard to raise us all with love and opportunity. I love them, but these children are too important to me. They are my family now," she said.

Brooks didn't know how to respond to that. She'd been raised with love and opportunity and was trying to give the same to these children who had none of that. He gave money because it eased the guilt of not being able to interact with children who had been through trauma like him, but the only little people he ever enjoyed being around were Zack and Maddie's kids. He'd grown to love Chalise, Izzy, and Alex, but children who didn't have families made him uncomfortable. No, uncomfortable wasn't strong enough. The very word *orphan* brought a cold sweat to his forehead and reminded him of the misery, darkness, and fear of his youth. He couldn't go back there.

"How's your pasta?" he asked.

"It's wonderful. Thank you." Sydnee's eyes narrowed, but thankfully she didn't comment on the redirection.

"Thank you for giving me a chance to impress you."

She laughed, and he realized that he couldn't risk a follow-up date with this woman, no matter how badly he wanted to kiss her. She was much too caring and made him remember all the things he used to believe he wanted out of life. Stability, charity for others, love. He had a good life with friends who worked for and with him, dating different women on the island, and tourists who came in on the ships. He'd flirt, laugh, spoil the ladies with gifts, and then kiss them goodbye. He wasn't ready for a woman who had so much ... heart. His heart and life had been shattered at five years old. He wasn't going to rebuild it at thirty-two.

CHAPTER FIVE

Brooks's business partner, Evelyn, was the closest thing to a mother he'd ever known. As he walked out of the security area of the airport, he saw her waiting for him in her standard silk shirt and dress pants. Her once-smooth skin showed a few age spots and smile wrinkles, but she looked as put together as usual.

"You flew commercial?" was her first question after she released him from a long hug.

"I've got this girl who's driving me nuts, making me rethink everything, and for some reason I felt guilty chartering a flight."

Evelyn's perfectly plucked and dyed brows squiggled. "Brooks, you have a different girl every other day. You're actually allowing one to affect you?"

"No." He shook his head vehemently and hefted his bag into the trunk of her Lexus. He'd spent most of the flight trying to focus on the meetings he needed to attend over the next week, but Sydnee kept intruding on his thoughts. "No," he said again.

"Methinks you protest too much," Evelyn said lightly.

Brooks opened the passenger door and escorted her in. He shut it, then walked around to the opposite side of the car. Evelyn didn't mind driving, but he knew she preferred that he navigate through Fresno's busy traffic. They talked about the company they were acquiring as he steered the car toward his estate outside the city.

Darren was on guard duty and welcomed him home as he opened the security gate.

Brooks drove the car expertly onto the front circle, and looked up at the three-story mansion his adoptive father had bestowed on him ten years ago, along with more money than Brooks could ever spend. He tried to be a wise executor of the estate, but Evelyn basically ran everything and seemed to enjoy it. After graduating with a master's degree and learning all the ins and outs of his businesses, he'd relocated to Cozumel to give her the space to expand their business and investments the way she wanted without him constantly looking over her shoulder. He wondered how he'd manage everything when she decided to retire.

He jumped from the vehicle and hurried around to get her door.

"Thank you." She patted his cheek.

Brooks couldn't resist pulling her into a hug again. She was tall and still in good shape for a sixty-year-old woman.

"You miss him?" she guessed.

"Always."

"He would've been very proud of you."

Brooks tilted his head and eyed her. "Would he?"

"Yes. You're a good man, Brooks." A twinkle appeared in her blue eyes. "The only thing that would make both of us prouder is if you'd settle down and have babies."

Babies. The very word could induce a panic attack. Settling down was one of those phrases he hated to hear, especially out of someone he loved and respected as much as Evelyn.

She laughed. "You should see your face."

They walked slowly up the wide sidewalk, trimmed with Mr. Hoffman's prized rose bushes. Evelyn kept the maintenance crews busy taking good care of the mansion, but she hadn't changed paint colors or furniture since Mr. Hoffman had passed.

After walking through the grand entry, they headed straight for the kitchen. Lou-Lou was whipping something up on the stove that smelled strongly of spicy Cajun seasoning. *Oh, yes.*

She saw Brooks, squealed, and dropped the spatula. Brooks hurried to meet her, picking her up off her feet and swinging the round woman in a circle.

"Laws, son," she tittered. "You get bigger every time I see you. Guess I'd better cook double."

"Yes, you should." Brooks released her, and she immediately turned to the fridge and got him a glass of lemonade.

Mr. Hoffman had found Lou-Lou in the slums of Oakland only a handful of blocks from where he'd found Brooks. They were all family now, and though Lou-Lou's dark-brown skin was wrinkling, she didn't look like she'd aged much in the past twenty years. Brooks hoped she and Evelyn would live forever. It was hard enough to lose Mr. Hoffman.

"Let's take our drinks out back," Evelyn suggested.

Brooks loved this part of coming home. Talking with Evelyn, knowing Lou-Lou was cooking all of his favorites. He felt like a teenage boy with no worries. He needed a mirror to make sure the acne hadn't returned.

They settled into plush chairs on the beautiful rock-inlaid patio overlooking the gardens and pool.

"I miss him too," Evelyn admitted after a few minutes of listening to the birds twitter and the wind rustle through the acres of grape vines that spread out beyond the two acres of grass, trees, and flower gardens.

Brooks turned his shoulders to focus on her. "Why didn't you ever marry him?" The question had never occurred to him until the past couple of days, when he couldn't get Sydnee and crazy thoughts of settling down out of his mind. Why hadn't Mr. Hoffman ever remarried? Especially when it was obvious how much he and Evelyn cared for each other.

Evelyn took a prim sip of her drink, sighed, forced a smile, and whispered, "I did marry him."

"*What?*" Brooks dropped his drink. It splattered across his shoes and the patio. He jumped up and started toward the house. He'd find something to clean this mess up and hide out until he was ready to deal with Evelyn's revelation.

"Sit down," Evelyn instructed. "James will wash off the patio, and Angelina can clean your shoes later."

Brooks stared down at her.

"Sit, Brooks. Your face is much too expressive today." She smiled benevolently at him. "What am I saying? Your face is always expressive."

"When?" He sat, but felt coiled like a tiger ready to spring.

"We loved each other for years."

"I know." He swallowed and admitted, "I always thought of you as my mom."

"Thank you." She nodded and squeezed his hand. "I wanted to be there for you all the time, but after the fiasco with his first wife ..." She shook her head. "It took him years to buy her off and legally bind her from ever acquiring his assets."

Brooks nodded; he knew about all of this. Mr. Hoffman's first wife had been horrific. It'd cost several million dollars and legal fees nobody wanted to remember, but she could never touch Mr. Hoffman's, now Brooks', money.

"He loved you so much." Evelyn wiped away a tear.

Brooks had to look down, lest he cry himself. The man who had rescued him and raised him had been strict and proper enough that Brooks never even called him dad, but he still knew that his adoptive father had loved him.

"When did you marry him?" he finally drummed up the courage to ask again. He felt slighted that he hadn't known. He was their child. Sort of.

"When you were eighteen, we did it in a secret ceremony."

"Why wouldn't he give you his name? Tell the world?" *Tell me?* He clenched his fist.

Evelyn took another sip of her drink. "I also have a horrible ex-husband and a daughter who I'd be embarrassed for you to meet. If either of them caught wind of the money I was part of, they would leech on to you like nothing you've ever seen."

"Mr. Hoffman was brilliant. He could've set things up to protect the money." There was so much they hadn't told him. Why? Couldn't he be trusted?

She shrugged. "He did set up legal paths that would protect you, but we both felt it would ensure less headache and stress in your future if no one ever found out we were married."

"Why was he so concerned about protecting me?" Brooks scuffed his dirty shoe along the brick patio. "I'm nobody."

Evelyn gripped his hands so hard it hurt. "Don't you ever say that again. You were everything to him, and you're everything to me. I love you so much ... son."

Brooks stood and pulled her up, gathering her into his arms. From living on the streets, being a gang member, and almost being killed in a knife fight in Oakland at ten years old, to this mansion and Mr. Hoffman and Evelyn loving him. He was truly blessed. What would Sydnee think if she knew about his past? She'd warmed considerably after she found out he was Christian. His adoptive father had hidden a wife so that Brooks could have every opportunity in the world. Would Brooks be that selfless for a child, for anyone? He really didn't think so.

CHAPTER SIX

"Tag, you're it!" Sydnee screamed. She dodged away from Mario, but Daniel and Alejandro sandwiched her between them. She cried out in protest, but they held on to her until six-year-old Mario could tag her. Sydnee dropped to the grass and pulled them down with her. It quickly turned into a wrestling match.

She had discovered one thing about boys that no human development class had fully prepared her for. They needed to get out their aggression, and it was much better to do it with innocent games, sports, and wrestling. They also needed physical touch, but didn't usually want to admit it. Impromptu wrestling matches killed two birds with one stone. Daniel launched onto her back, about knocking her to the ground. He was the oldest boy, and he'd had a growth spurt the past few months—he definitely outweighed her and was almost as tall. She had a pretty good grip on Alejandro and was tickling his armpits when she heard her name.

"Sydnee? Camila needs you to run into the shopping center. She's got a list."

The boys groaned and pushed to their feet to help Sydnee up. "Why me? She usually does the errands."

"She said she's too busy today and thought you could use the break."

Sydnee hadn't left the home since her date with Brooks two weeks ago. He hadn't come by or contacted her; he simply deposited her at the orphanage that night with a handshake, a devastatingly handsome smile, and a thank-you. She'd gone on the date planning to tell him off and offend him so he'd leave her alone, but she'd changed her mind between the shrimp and the tres leches. She enjoyed talking with him and loved the way he treated everyone around him.

Now she really wanted to get to know him better. If he had tried some of his romantic moves at the end of the date instead of the beginning, she would've stood on tiptoes and kissed him until his staff pulled them apart. But he hadn't, and luckily, the kiddos had kept her busy the past two weeks so she could stay in her sheltered spot, doting on them and ignoring the fact that it hurt that Brooks wasn't interested. It hurt a lot. He'd probably dropped her like a hot rock because she hadn't draped herself all over him like every other woman. Christian? Yeah, right.

She left the boys playing soccer with Rosmerta and changed into a white tank top and a simple pink peasant skirt. She almost walked away without jewelry and touching up her makeup, but her mother's influence was too strong. Adding a long silver necklace and pale pink lipstick, she hopped into the low-rider pickup truck and slowly made her way into town. Many tourists out on scooters or in jeeps slowed her progress.

The truck was covered in rust spots, and they had to throw a blanket over the seats or sit on springs, but it ran well. She knew Brooks gave a whole dump truck full of money to the orphanage, but Camila was very smart and frugal. They didn't drive nice vehicles or eat steak every night. Camila put a lot of money away in case of emergencies—emergencies meaning Brooks deciding not to help them anymore. Sydnee kept worrying after the date that he would pull his sponsorship, but Camila hadn't said a word about it, and she would have been a stress case if that had happened.

Sydnee parked behind the open market. The streets were packed today, the high smoke stacks and spires of two cruise ships looming over the port. Sydnee didn't mind the crowds. It always made her smile to see people from all over the world descend on the little island and enjoy themselves.

The clothes in the tourist shops were actually reasonably priced, and the shopkeepers gave locals a discount, so Camila, Rosmerta, and Sydnee always supported them rather than ordering online. Sydnee walked past the shop where she'd first met Brooks and smiled wistfully. She couldn't resist going inside.

Perusing some beautiful scarves, she suddenly felt his presence. Warm, spicy sandalwood scent and the arrival of all man. She smiled and kept looking forward, hoping beyond hope that he would flirt with her.

"Did you come to this store again just aching to see me, love?"

Sydnee bit at her lip to keep from cheering. "Maybe." She glanced over at him and caught a breath. He was more handsome than he'd been two weeks ago. She was sure of it. His hair had been trimmed, but he had a couple days' growth on his strong jaw. Instead of hiding his beautifully formed lips, the dark hair accented them. His deep brown eyes sparkled mischievously at her.

"Maybe I should make something of this opportunity then," he murmured.

"I'm actually working, shopping for clothes for some of the girls." She tried to keep her head clear and focus on why she was here, but it was difficult with him looking at her like that.

"You work too much." Brooks brushed a lock of hair over her shoulder, his fingers tiptoeing over her bare skin. "Last time I checked, I paid your salary." He grinned. "That means you work for me, and as your boss, I recommend you should take some time off."

Sydnee turned to face him more fully. She'd been dying to see him, but she didn't know if she liked the idea that she worked for him. What if he tried to manipulate the situation? "What do you want me to do with my time?" she asked much too breathlessly.

His lips turned up in the most irresistible grin. Were his teeth always that white? A man that took such good care of his pearly whites would probably taste really, really good. Dang. Her imagination was running wild.

"Spend it making this big guy happy."

Sydnee caught a breath. "I don't even know what would make you happy."

He rested a hand on the wall behind her and leaned in. His breath was tinged with cinnamon. Yes, those lips would taste as good as they looked. "I think being with you would do the trick."

"Then why haven't you called or stopped by? It's been two weeks." Oh, crap, she'd put that out there.

His eyes widened, and then a slow grin appeared. Sydnee had to hold on to the display rack for support. What was he doing to her? She'd been fine the past two weeks. She hadn't needed to see him, but now it all came back. His charm and grin were completely irresistible. There was no way to claim that she was something special when she knew he was the type of guy that flirted with anything in a skirt. Why was she succumbing so easily?

"I had to fly home to Fresno and settle some business."

"The entire two weeks?" She shook her head. "I'm sorry. So Fresno's your home? Did you get to see your family?" She was a hot mess, more worried about him not seeing her than she was about how he was doing. She needed to get out of here, buy the girls' clothes, and rush to the safety of the orphanage.

"I did." His eyes clouded. "I don't really have family, but I visited with the women who raised me. Our housekeeper, Lou-Lou, and my business partner, Evelyn. Evelyn was actually married to my father, Mr. Hoffman. Well, my adopted father ..." His voice trailed off, and he stared over her head.

"Is your father ... gone?"

"Yes. Ten years ago."

Sydnee loved that he'd confided that to her. "I am very sorry for your loss, now and in the past."

Brooks focused in on her again. "Thank you. I don't usually share that kind of thing."

"With women?" Her back stiffened. She knew she was just another fling to him, but it still hurt to have him spell it out.

"With anyone." He cleared his throat. "To answer your first question, I wasn't gone the entire two weeks. I didn't feel it was fair to contact you again."

"Fair?" Why did he get to decide if it was fair or not?

He exhaled slowly. "You're not my usual type, Sydnee."

She bristled again, placing a hand on her hip and tossing her long hair. "You mean I'm not a floozy who kisses you the first time you stare into her eyes."

He pursed his lips and then nodded. "That's fair and kind of true. Most women want me, and they let me know that. You were feisty and prickly and unapproachable."

"Wow. Don't make me sound so desirable."

"You are definitely that too. All that Southern charm." He squeezed her hand gently. "I don't usually date any women for longer than one or two dates, a week at the most."

"Why?" He'd just admitted what a huge player he was. She should walk away, but she was too intrigued by him. He was opening up to her, and it sounded like that wasn't his usual mode of operation. She wanted to hear his story and his adoptive parents' story, and she really wanted to keep looking into his dark eyes and have his fingers touch her shoulder again.

Brooks studied her for half a minute. "Can I buy you a raspas?"

"Well, since you are my boss, you make it kind of hard for a girl to say no."

"That's what I like to hear." He rewarded her with a smile, placed a hand on her lower back, and directed her toward the open market. They got their ices from a vendor and found a bench to sit on. Sydnee leaned back and soaked in the sun, watching the tourists barter with shopkeepers.

She loved every minute of her life with the children, but sometimes it was nice to be outside and sit on a bench with nobody needing her. She glanced askance at Brooks. Well, except for the big guy next to her. He definitely seemed to need someone. He hadn't even called his father figure by anything but Mr. Hoffman. He apparently had an interesting past and family situation, but his staff seemed to be like relatives to him.

She licked the cool ice, savoring the fresh mango flavor. They sat in silence for a few minutes watching the people, enjoying the cold treat, and Sydnee really liked his shoulder brushing against hers. The too-confident man she'd met weeks ago had morphed into an intriguing and overly handsome puzzle.

"You were going to tell me why you only date women for a week?" *And why I'm special? Please say I'm special to you.*

"Do you want to go with me to my friend's island for a Thanksgiving party?" he blurted out. "Zack's island is like heaven ... very romantic." He grinned broadly at her.

"Excuse me?" *A singles party?* What a way to ruin Thanksgiving. She hated loud, dark, and yucky singles parties. Definitely not her version of romance.

He looked chagrined for the first time since she'd met him. "Bad idea? Can I talk you into thinking it's a good idea? You don't have to share a room with me."

Share a room? "No way! You just need to wait a Sam Hill minute."

"Sam Hill?"

"You said you were a Christian." She turned and poked a finger into his chest. "You lied to me so you could get me away to some island frat party?" She stood and stomped her foot. "How dare you? I've told ya once, I'll tell ya a thousand times: I'm *not* for sale and I'm not a floozy!"

Brooks's eyes were round. He didn't move from the bench. She whirled from him and stomped through the crowds to the truck. The anger started to dissipate, and she wondered if she'd overreacted. Why had she been so quick to accuse him? Should she rush back and give him a chance to explain? No! He had no right to try to take her to some island kegger and think she was going to be gung ho about it. What a liar. Why did he wear a cross and claim he was a Christian? What a stinking liar. Her stomach churned with frustration, and she had to brush a tear off her cheek.

Her steps slowed. She was taking this much too hard. Her reaction must be so strong because she hadn't dated much on the island and she was working long hours to take care of the kiddos, so she didn't take any time for herself. That had to be it. Brooks wasn't that special, and he definitely didn't think she was anything special.

It wasn't until she pulled into the orphanage with the tears on her cheeks finally drying that she remembered the clothes she was supposed to buy.

CHAPTER SEVEN

Brooks slammed a thirty-six-inch box onto the padded floor and leapt onto and off of it. He didn't have a clue why he'd opened himself up to Sydnee just so she could slam him to the curb. Ridiculous. There were dozens—no, there were hundreds of women wanting a piece of him. He didn't need her or her prickly misinterpretations of everything he said. He should fire her. That would serve her right. He paused to catch his breath.

No, he should pull his funding from the orphanage. His gut twisted with hunger pangs like he used to have as a boy. He'd never admitted to anyone that he lived in Cozumel to distance himself from his past, to never be cold or hungry again, and because hey, who didn't want to be king of their own island?

He could never do anything to harm those children. The reason he donated so much was to ensure any child on this island who had a need would be provided for and loved. The past couple of years he'd even funded college educations for three of the children who had graduated high school and wanted to go to the mainland for schooling. Several others now worked for him.

He thought of Sydnee again. She definitely loved those children. Why couldn't she love him?

Bah! He didn't need love. Especially from a vindictive, bitter woman.

He turned around and used the box as a platform to do a set of triceps dips. Sweat dripped into his eyes, and he blinked it away.

An idea came, and he couldn't help but grin. She believed he wanted to take advantage of her and force her into the equivalent of a drunken college kegger? Well, he'd make her believe it, giving her a good scare in the process.

She would regret being so rash and rude to him. He stood and stretched his arms behind his back, admiring the way his triceps bulged. Sydnee obviously wasn't interested in him, and he kept telling himself he didn't care, but he had the power to toy with her, then make her realize how wrong she'd been and how she shouldn't have insulted him with her assumptions. He rubbed his hands together and dialed Camila's number.

"Mr. Hoffman?" The woman never wasted any time.

"I have a favor to ask."

"Of course, sir, anything."

Brooks smiled. Sydnee was going on the trip to see Zack and Maddie with him, whether she liked it or not. He didn't know if he was going to focus on teaching her a lesson or convincing her to like him, but either way he was going to have fun.

CHAPTER EIGHT

S ydnee rose from her knees, exhausted. All she could think about was stretching out in her twin bed. The aches from Daniel accidentally tackling her in their impromptu soccer game might ease then. With any luck, she'd be asleep within minutes and none of the babies would awaken tonight. It was her night with the baby monitor.

She heard shouting in the back yard and leapt to her feet, rushing from her room in a tank top and shorts, not taking time to throw shoes on. Two steps down the hallway, Alejandro appeared in the back door frame. "Mees Sydnee, Mees Sydnee!" Alejandro tore toward her.

What on the Lord's green earth was going on? The boys had been asleep for an hour. At least that's what she thought.

He started spewing out words in Spanish and English. Her Spanish wasn't good enough to understand everything, but she caught, "Men ... Daniel ... taken."

Sydnee grabbed his arms. "Calm down. I can't understand. Someone took Daniel?"

"Sí!"

"Show me where." She tugged on his hand, and that was all the encouragement he needed to sprint for the back door.

Camila came out of her room, looking ticked at the noise after bedtime. "What—"

"Daniel's been taken," Sydnee shot at her as they ran past. "Call the police."

"The police won't help," Camila said.

Sydnee's breath caught. Camila was probably right. If this was a group of traffickers, the police would probably look the other way, especially if it was a child without family support. Her experience with the police was that they followed the laws of the land, unless extreme amounts of money were involved. Trafficking was huge money. Why did they take Daniel and leave Alejandro? Maybe because Daniel was bigger, and they could sell him as a worker?

She and Alejandro tore into the night and out into the trees behind the property. She could hear signs of a struggle up ahead. There was a road to the north. They must've parked their vehicle and cut through to the back of the property. How in the world was she going to take on traffickers with no weapon and in a tank top, shorts, and no shoes?

There was a decent moon, so she could see where she was going. The terrain quickly changed from the soft grass of their backyard to jungle. Trees thicker than Momma's gravy batted at her as if they were determined to keep her from protecting one of her boys. Sydnee's feet were poked and slit by broken branches and rocks, but she didn't slow down. As they got closer to the sounds of several people banging through the undergrowth, she turned to Alejandro. "Go back! I'll help Daniel."

"No! Daniel fight so I can escape. I fight for him."

Sydnee knew this ten-year-old boy wouldn't be able to fight against full-grown men. It was a miracle Daniel was giving them the resistance it sounded like he was, and they hadn't already loaded him into a truck and disappeared.

"Go back!" she commanded, then sprinted toward the fight. There was no need to cover her approach; they were loud enough.

Branches whipped at her face as she reached a clearing next to the road. Three men had Daniel by the arms and legs, but they couldn't completely restrain him. He used whatever limb he was able to free from their grasp to hit or kick them. His long, thin body writhed and bucked like a wild bronco. The men had their hands full trying to get him to the truck that was parked on the road. None of them saw Sydnee coming.

She launched herself onto the nearest man's back, wrapped her arms securely around his throat, and threw her body weight backward. He released Daniel and they slammed to the ground. The man didn't appear much bigger than her, but his weight on top of her was suffocating. Sydnee held on for all she was worth. Her older brother was a Marine and had taught her if she could lock her arms and hold on long enough, she could make a full-grown man pass out.

The man thrashed on top of her and she thought she was going to pass out herself from his raunchy, sweaty smell and the pressure of his body grinding her back into the uneven, rocky ground. She screamed and kept her elbow locked tight around his throat even as his fingers clawed at her. His movements became slower, then suddenly he was dead weight on top of her.

Sydnee groaned and pushed out from under him. Daniel scratched and clawed at the man holding him. The other man had Alejandro under one arm and a knife to the boy's throat. They were all shouting in Spanish, and Sydnee had no clue what they were saying or how to save the little boy. She should've known Alejandro would follow her. Why hadn't she forced the boy to turn back earlier or made Camila grab him? Dumb! What if this man cut him open?

She climbed to her feet with her hands splayed. "Please. Let them go. You can take me."

Daniel stopped fighting and screamed, "No!"

"Yes." Sydnee made eye contact with Daniel, then gestured toward Alejandro. The little boy was quivering in fear. The man holding him had an evil look in his black eyes. From his scarred cheek to his deeply slanting brows, he simply had the hardened appearance of a criminal. He pushed the knife harder. Alejandro let out the most heartrending scream of pain and blood trickled down his throat.

"No!" Sydnee screamed, launching herself across the small clearing.

"Back," the man commanded.

Sydnee stopped a few feet away, realizing that Alejandro had a small cut but wasn't dead. Her heart thudded against her chest, and she couldn't draw a full breath. Her boys! She had to save them. She wanted to talk fast to convince the traffickers to take her and leave the boys, but didn't know how much English they understood and she knew Daniel wouldn't translate. He was alternating between glaring at their captors defiantly and his eyes filling with terror as he looked at his friend.

"Take me." Sydnee pointed to herself. "More money for me."

"We aren't stupid," the man holding Alejandro said, his eyes sweeping over her body.

Sydnee was relieved he could understand, but the coldness of his voice shot tremors through her body. She would be sacrificing herself in every manner for her boys.

"Good," she said. "Then you'll recognize that you'd get a lot more money selling me than these boys." A huge portion of human trafficking was the porn and sex industry. Sydnee's stomach convulsed at the thought. She forced future fears away. Maybe she could fight her way free after Daniel and Alejandro were safe. Maybe.

The man restraining Daniel watched them questioningly. He didn't seem to understand what they were saying, and the man holding Alejandro was obviously the leader. Sydnee heard a groan behind her. The guy she'd knocked out was reviving. She had to act fast.

She took a large step closer. "Take me," she demanded.

The man's eyes gleamed. He moved the knife from Alejandro's throat and threw the boy to the ground. Grabbing Sydnee's arm, he flung her against his chest and placed the knife against her skin. He pushed his nose close to her neck and inhaled. Her stomach convulsed at his touch and the reek of his foul breath.

"Umm," he moaned. "Much better trade."

Sydnee swallowed back bile, goose bumps rising on her flesh. The cold steel against her neck and this hardened man's arms around her was a terror she'd never experienced. Alejandro stood slowly and backed away.

"Run," she mouthed to him.

He shook his head. Daniel renewed his efforts to free himself from his captor.

"Calm down or I slice her open," the man holding Sydnee said.

Sydnee drew in a quick breath. He wouldn't kill her. She was worth too much alive. She had to believe that or she would pass out from the fear.

Daniel stopped fighting, his eyes desperate as he looked at her. "Mees Sydnee," he whispered.

Sydnee loved him so much in that moment. He would've sacrificed himself for her like he'd already tried to do for Alejandro.

"Mees Sydnee," the man mocked. "Beautiful American trying to help the poor orphans. Yes, you'll bring me a lot of money."

"Let him go. You have me," she commanded with a slightly quavering voice.

The man laughed. "You are a dumb negotiator." He started tugging her toward the truck.

A large form appeared at the edge of the clearing. The man holding her jerked to a stop. The newcomer stepped closer, and Sydnee gasped. Brooks. He was dressed all in black with a gun slung over his back and a wicked knife in his hand. He looked terrifying. She'd never seen a more welcome or attractive sight.

His eyes swept over her, then hardened as they focused on the man holding her. "Let her go and I will kill you quickly."

The man laughed, but it was unsteady. "As opposed to what?"

"Slicing you up slowly and savoring every minute of it."

Sydnee swallowed hard. From the look on Brooks's face, he wasn't bluffing.

"I'll slice her open right now," the man threatened. The edge of his knife grazed Sydnee's neck. She flinched away from it. How could Brooks save her with the position she was in?

Brooks threw the knife before her mind had even recognized his hand was in motion. The man's arm jerked. He screamed and dropped his knife, Brooks's weapon embedded in his upper arm. His arm around her slackened, and Sydnee dodged out of his grasp.

Brooks flew across the clearing and knocked the man to the ground in one punch. José grabbed the man holding Daniel, who seemed to be in shock. She had no clue where José had even appeared from.

Daniel rushed to Sydnee and wrapped his arms around her waist. Alejandro knocked into her other side an instant later.

Sydnee held the boys close, and she thought she murmured comforting words, but all she could do was stare at Brooks as he hauled the man to his feet. Blood streamed down the man's arm from the knife still protruding out of his flesh, but he didn't complain or act like he even hurt. He kept looking at Sydnee even as Brooks yanked the knife out, then pulled his arms behind his back and held him as José tied his wrists.

The third man sat up, but José had him hog-tied before he could make a fuss. Brooks pushed all three men down to the ground and nodded to José, who had a curved-bladed saber trained on them.

"You got them until the police get here?" Brooks asked.

"Yes, sir."

"Don't call me sir." Brooks clapped his friend on the shoulder, shoved his knife onto his belt, then started toward Sydnee and her boys. His eyes were filled with concern, but also had this predatory gleam in them. She took an instinctive step back and held on tightly to the boys.

Daniel stared up at Brooks and moved to stand in front of Sydnee.

"It's okay," Sydnee told him. "He's a good guy."

Alejandro clung to her. Daniel's eyes never left Brooks's face.

Brooks glanced at each of the boys, swallowed hard, and focused on Sydnee. "Are you okay?"

"Thanks to you," she managed to get out. She wanted to be the damsel in distress and fling herself into his very inviting arms, maybe even express her gratitude with a kiss, but she'd left things pretty awkward between them with her accusations and refusal to accompany him to his singles party. She didn't know how Brooks would react to her now. Yet he had saved her, and she would never forget that.

Brooks's eyes swept over her body as if reassuring himself she wasn't injured. "Let's get you all home." He took her elbow and gently escorted her toward the road as Alejandro held on to her other hand,

and Daniel stayed behind them like a protective little escort. How she loved these boys.

She stubbed her toe on a large rock, and a little gasp of pain escaped. Brooks stopped. "You okay?" His voice was so tender. She'd seen the overconfident womanizer and now the warrior, but this tender side was something new, and she was more drawn to him than she'd ever been to a man.

"Yes." She didn't want to look like a wimp. "Stubbed my toe."

He glanced down her bare legs to her unshod feet. "Aha. I knew you wanted an excuse to be back in my arms." He grinned. "Honestly, woman. All you had to do was ask."

"What?" Sydnee had barely released the question when Brooks let go of her elbow and swept her up into his arms. All her air whooshed out as she was cradled against his muscular chest, her lips inches from his strong jawline. If she arched up a little bit, she could see if that day's growth was soft or stubbly. It sure made him look rugged and much too manly.

He smelled good, clean and kind of spicy, a wonderful contrast to the foul sweat of the traffickers. Glancing down at her, he smiled. "What?"

"Nothing." She blushed, hoping he hadn't guessed where her thoughts were. Their interactions had been fire and ice, and she didn't need to have him thinking she wanted him like every other female seemed to.

"You had that look," he said quietly so the boys didn't overhear them.

"What look?" she whispered back.

"Like you might've changed your mind and want a piece of all of this."

Sydnee stiffened. He had noticed where her thoughts were leading her. "Don't get your hopes up, big guy."

"Oh, I will." Brooks chuckled and tucked her in closer to his body.

It was hard to resist cuddling into him. He felt wonderful against her, especially after being so terrified of what the traffickers would do to her and the boys, and what their fate would've been if Brooks hadn't appeared looking like a dark-haired Thor coming to their rescue. All he needed was the hammer. She licked her lips.

The bright lights of the orphanage beaconed ahead. Rosmerta, Camila, and Daniel and Alejandro's little buddy, Mario, waited on the steps. Their faces lit up when they saw them, and they started running in their direction. A couple of police cars raced up. Brooks set her on her feet when they reached the grass and went to stow his weapons in his Hummer. In all the confusion, she didn't even get a chance to thank him.

CHAPTER NINE

The older children were still at school on the Wednesday before Thanksgiving, and Sydnee was enjoying holding baby Tomás, rocking away while he slurped down his bottle. She kissed his forehead and savored the smell of lotion and clean baby. She felt a rush of affection for this innocent boy. Would she really experience more maternal love than this for her own children? Her sisters and mom assured her she would, but she didn't know how it could be possible.

Thanksgiving was tomorrow, and she ached for her nieces and nephews. That was the problem with being part of a huge, loving family: too many people to love and miss when you were away. She glanced down at the precious baby. Her spot was here, but sometimes she wondered if this was what her life was always going to be. She couldn't imagine ever leaving, but if she didn't, would she marry or have her own children? Her focus needed to be on loving all of these children who needed her so badly. It was almost like being a nun. She laughed at the comparison, though sadly, it wasn't far off.

Sobering quickly, she blinked back tears. She had cried several times since that awful night when Brooks had rescued them. She wished he'd ask her to go to Thanksgiving at his friend's island again. This time she might say yes, even if it was a drunken party he was taking her to. No, she reprimanded herself. Good Southern Christian girls didn't lower their standards.

"Sydnee?" Rosmerta's call rang through the building, and Julio started crying in his crib.

She lifted Tomás onto her chest to burp him.

"There you are." Rosmerta rushed into the room and picked up Julio, rocking and singing until the baby was cooing. "Camila needs you in her office right away."

Tomás let out a large burp, and they both laughed. "Wow. Guess he didn't want to make Camila wait." Sydnee swaddled the baby and lay him down for his afternoon nap. She whispered goodbye to Rosmerta, who almost had Julio back to sleep, and slowly made her way to Camila's office. Rapping her knuckles on the door, she waited.

"Oh, good, you're here." Camila didn't even invite her in, but took her arm and pulled her down the hallway toward the bedrooms. "You need to pack. Mr. Hoffman has requested that you accompany him on his yacht to a private island for Thanksgiving."

"What?" Sydnee stopped in the hallway and yanked her arm free. Warmth started in the pit of her stomach and worked its way out. Brooks wanted her with him. She would get a chance to thank him. Would he want a kiss of gratitude? Probably more than a kiss. As quick as the joy started, it diffused. He wanted her to be one of his hoochie mommas at some party. Would she have to watch as he flirted with other women? While they flirted with him? That thought made her stomach roll. How dare he get to her through her boss after she'd already blatantly told him no. The rescue might make her ache for him, but it couldn't change her value system. "I told him no. I'm not going anywhere with that man."

Camila sighed heavily. "You go, or he pulls his funding from the orphanage."

Sydnee's heart sank. It was exactly what she'd feared and the kind of stunt she thought Brooks was capable of when she first met him. She really wanted to believe that the Brooks she'd gotten to know a little bit wouldn't do something like this. "So you're going to prostitute me?" Just saying that made her feel filthy.

"I am not!" Camila gasped, looking properly offended. "Who said anything about sleeping with him?"

"A man doesn't invite you on a yacht and to a private island without expecting some side benefits," Sydnee said heavily.

"Sydnee, I've known Mr. Hoffman for five years now."

"Wait. You've known him for five years, and I've never met him before?"

"I hadn't met him myself until the other day. I've known him through phone calls, emails, and word of mouth for five years. He's obviously interested in you, but I can promise you he is a good man and would never force himself on a woman. If you don't want to sleep with him, just say no."

"Right, and then he pulls our funding whether I go on the trip or not."

Camila grabbed her shoulders. "My sister-in-law cleans Mr. Hoffman's house, and her cousin, José, is his personal assistant and close friend. He dates a lot of women, that's true, but they never stay the night. José told me that sometimes they beg, and Mr. Hoffman just charms them and sends them away."

Sydnee's eyes narrowed. Camila had obviously been drinking the Brooks's Kool-Aid and was desperate to keep their funding. Sydnee felt the same way about the funding, and though she might be able to believe Brooks wasn't sleeping around, how was she going to stay strong being around him for an entire weekend? Especially when visions of him fighting for her and the boys came to mind.

"Please, Sydnee," Camila begged. "Who's going to hold little baby Tomás when you and I have to get jobs to provide enough food for the children here? Forget about clothing, medical supplies, schooling, or opportunities to leave the island. Are you going to be the one to tell Daniel he can't play soccer anymore? To stop Alejandro's wrestling lessons? To pull María out of her tumbling classes? To put these children at even more risk of traffickers stealing them? They'll be lucky to have a place to live, and Daniel and Alejandro will have to take care of the babies so we can go work or scrounge up food."

Sydnee's stomach was lead. How could Brooks put her in this position? Was she supposed to be some high-dollar escort? *Humiliating.* He knew she'd cave because he knew how much she loved these children. The children. If she'd been willing to go with the traffickers and submit to whatever torture they had in mind to protect them, she should be able to handle spending a weekend with this infuriating, selfish, and unfortunately, beautiful, man. She'd go and maybe get a chance to wring his treacherous neck.

"Okay," she muttered.

"Okay?" Camila's voice squeaked.

"I'll do it. If he'll promise not to touch me or try any of his romantic crap." One look and he had her quivering at the knees. How was she going to keep from succumbing to his tricks on a private yacht and a private island? He'd said a Thanksgiving party on his friend's island. Images of a crazy party with a bunch of single people kept plaguing her. She was so not into that scene. What happened to turkey and dressing and pumpkin pie for Thanksgiving? Instead she was headed for spring break debauchery.

Camila laughed. "I'm sure by the end of the trip you'll be begging him to touch you. Can you believe how good-looking he is and so rich and funny too?"

Sydnee rolled her eyes. "Just tell him my terms or I'm not going."

"Fine. You go pack and I'll let him know."

"You'll call him?"

"No. He's waiting right outside."

Sydnee's palms started sweating. Brooks was outside. Right now? Part of her wanted to touch up her makeup and go talk to him, finally give him a proper thank-you for rescuing them. But, the sane part of her wanted to go knee him where it hurts for placing her in this situation. She dragged her feet to her bedroom and packed quickly. Maybe the good Lord would see fit to protect her from Brooks's charm. Hopefully some of the people on the island would be tolerable to be around.

She stopped by the nursery to kiss the babies, lingering over Tomás's crib. He looked so adorable lying on his stomach with his tush in the air and his cheek squished against the sheet. How was she going stay away from him for almost four days? Forcing herself to leave after one last kiss on the cheek, she went out the backdoor and hugged each of the toddlers on the playset with Rosmerta. Her friend gave her a quick side squeeze. "Have fun, and give that handsome guy a kiss for me, eh?"

"There will be no kissing," Sydnee insisted. "Can you tell all the big kiddos that I'll be back Sunday, and I miss and love them? Especially Daniel and Alejandro." The boys had only left her side for school and bedtime the past few days. They'd all bonded together, and after seeing how determined they were to protect her, she knew she would do anything for them.

"Yes, yes, they'll be fine without you."

"Will you? It's going to be busy with only the two of you."

"Mr. Hoffman is sending some of his house staff to help since he won't be home this weekend. We'll have so much extra help, I won't have to scrub a toilet or clean a dish all weekend." She winked. "Now have fun! You deserve a vacation."

Sydnee forced a smile so her friend wouldn't worry. She walked around the side of the house. Brooks stood next to his black Hummer, studying the front door like it was the key to his happiness. He clenched and unclenched his fist. Then he ran his hand through his hair. She noticed he was clean shaven today, and his stretchy V-neck shirt and gray pants fit all too well. He looked ... really good. It wasn't fair for one man to have all those good looks but be a snake underneath. He'd basically committed extortion with Camila. Anger rose up until it was almost choking her. She walked his direction.

He turned at the sound of her footsteps and his face lit up. "Sydnee!" Rushing to her, he took her bag and gave her a hug. Sydnee barely had time to process those strong arms wrapped around her, those bulging chest muscles pressing against her shoulder, and that spicy sandalwood scent making her mouth water before he pulled away. "Thank you for coming with me. It's going to be great."

Sydnee blinked up at him. What was he talking about? "I didn't really have much choice."

"Why?" he asked.

"Camila said I go with you or you cut our funding." She tilted her head to the side and folded her arms across her chest. "Did she have a misunderstanding of some kind?"

Brooks gave a strangled sort of laugh, and a veil seemed to cover his face. His eyes lost their sparkle and he looked her over like a tiger stalking its dinner. "No, that was right." He took a step closer, and though he wasn't touching her, the strength and warmth of his body overshadowed her. "Did she tell you the other parameters?"

"That you won't touch or proposition me?"

He chuckled, and it was a dark, lifeless sound. "Don't worry. By the end of the trip you'll be begging me to touch and proposition you."

"In your dreams, big boy." She stomped around him, and José was there to open her door. Sliding into the seat, she sighed heavily. Who was Brooks, really? Her rescuer or her slaver? This was going to be a very long weekend with Dr. Jekyll and Mr. Hyde.

CHAPTER TEN

Brooks watched Sydnee closely as they walked onto his yacht, appreciating the way she filled out her clingy knee-length blue dress, but really wanting to see her reaction to his Ferretti. Her jaw dropped slightly, and she glanced back at him. "This is really nice."

"Only the best for you, ma'am." He bowed.

She smirked at his fake Southern accent.

He was relieved that she wasn't snipping at him. He'd hated seeing her in danger the other night. After he saved her life, he thought she might convert to a sweet woman and give him the obligatory kiss of gratitude, but no, not Sydnee. She was back to acting like he was the big bad wolf intent on compromising the innocent girl. He'd initially thought he might ham up that angle, but after seeing her with that knife against her neck, he couldn't stand the thought of her being in danger or pain. He loved the way she'd gazed at him like some kind of hero, and he'd considered telling Camila he'd changed his mind and didn't want to force her to come this weekend. It was pretty harsh to dangle the funding over their heads, yet it ticked him off that she believed he would actually pull it.

If Sydnee knew him, she'd know he would never do that to those children, but he realized she didn't know him. At all. She had a preconceived notion of him and believed what she wanted to believe, and despite himself, he really wanted to change her views.

He wondered for a second how he'd gotten into a misunderstood relationship with a beautiful woman who he wasn't ready to let go. Usually he got bored with women after a date or two, and he never let himself lose his cool or play dirty. Even with all he'd gone through in his youth, he wasn't vindictive. He was the happy-go-lucky "everything's good and everybody's my friend" kind of guy. True, that wasn't the deep down him, but he put on a pretty good act if he did say so himself. This woman had gotten him riled like no one had in years. Nothing seemed to bother him as much as this blonde, Southern sweetheart. And he used sweetheart in the loosest of terms.

José walked past them with Sydnee's bag and carried it down the stairs.

"Where's he taking my stuff?" Sydnee asked.

"To your ..." Brooks paused and he felt a surge of mischievousness. Why not rile her a little bit? "To the master suite."

Sydnee whirled on him, stepping close and poking a cute little finger in his face. "I was very specific that you are not even to touch me. What on the green earth would lead you to believe I would sleep with you?"

Brooks pasted on his best innocent expression. "My bags are in the guest suite, love." He cocked his head to the side, pasting on a feigned look of shock. No need to tell her they wouldn't even be sleeping on the yacht. "I already told you about my Christian values, but I guess *you* wanted to share the master?"

Sydnee looked embarrassed for half a second, but then the fire returned. "I want you to leave me alone so I can enjoy this beautiful boat."

"Y'all like my little Ferretti, eh? Well, sit back and enjoy the ride. If you get the hankering to serve me some hand-squeezed lemonade, give me a back rub, or sit on my lap, I'll be right over there." He pointed toward the captain's chair.

She whirled and stomped off to the back patio. Brooks didn't mind admiring the view, but hoped she wouldn't stay back there the entire ride. The only time he liked to be alone was when he exercised or fought.

José came back up the stairs and shook his hand. "You need anything else, boss?"

"Just throw in the lines, and I think we'll be good. Thank you, José. Give yourself a raise, will you?"

José grinned. "I already make more than any man I know, sir."

"Call me sir again and I'll dock your pay." Brooks really did hate to be called sir, and José knew it. Reminded him too much of his adoptive father and all the formality. That was to be expected of someone who came from a long line of British royals, but it meant that Brooks had never felt fully comfortable around Mr. Hoffman. On his deathbed, he'd finally told Brooks he loved him and asked him to call him father instead of Mr. Hoffman. A little late, but still Brooks owed the man everything.

José laughed.

"I'll see you in a few days."

José saluted and walked onto the boat ramp. He untied the yacht, and Brooks sauntered to the captain's chair. Gazing out back, he saw Sydnee stretched out on a chaise lounge with her nicely formed legs on fine display. He put his sunglasses on and grinned. It was going to be an entertaining weekend. That was for sure.

Sydnee watched the island of Cozumel fade into the distance. She wasn't sure if she was more upset with Camila, herself, or Brooks. He was the easiest one to take it out on, but she didn't know if he truly deserved it or not. He'd seemed like such a good guy the night he fed her dinner at his house and the other night when he'd rescued them. The hero of every woman's dreams, really.

What was she saying? He'd manipulated her aboard his yacht to take her to some frat party. She glanced around at the plush patio furniture, all white leather and dark wood. The yacht was beautiful. She'd never really understood wealthy people or boys and their toys. How could someone have a boat like this at their disposal and not realize it was excessive? The thing had to cost millions. Think of all the children he could help if he sold this thing. She sighed. He was self-funding the orphanage she'd committed herself to. Probably not a good idea to disparage him for not doing more.

It was a warm day on the water, and even with the ocean breeze, she was getting increasingly thirsty. She waited as long as she could, then decided she could handle a little more teasing from Brooks. She stood and stretched, then walked across the boat and into the galley. Opening the fridge, she retrieved three water bottles. She could at least try to play nice, whether Brooks deserved it or not. It was going to be a long weekend if she kept biting his head off whenever they talked.

Meandering to the captain chairs, she tried to act casual. "You want a bottle of water?"

"Oh yes, thank you." He brushed her hand as he took the bottle, then pointed to the seat next to him. "Would you do me the honor?"

Sydnee pried her eyes away from his handsome face and mischievous gaze. What was he planning to do with her? Why was he so insistent she go with him when she was frustrated with him or herself a good majority of the time they were together?

She glanced around. "Where's José?" She held aloft the third bottle. "In Cozumel."

Sydnee had started to settle into the chair. She bounced back up. "What? I thought he was coming with us."

"No. He's got things to do at home. His wife is expecting their second baby in December, and that woman is not happy when she's pregnant." He whistled. "She's a doll any other time, but something about pregnancy hormones." He shrugged. "I don't really get it."

Sydnee sat back down, placed both bottles in the cup holders, and concentrated on a few breaths. She was alone, on this gorgeous boat, with an even more gorgeous man. What was she going to do? "I didn't know José was married."

"Yeah. He has a cute little family."

"You just said cute." She eyed his large frame. "It doesn't really fit, ya know?"

Brooks smiled. "I call it like it is."

"Oh really? You've called me beautiful a few times." Darn it. That was fishing for a compliment like nothing.

His eyes slowly perused her body, landing on her face. "I call it like it is. You are exquisitely beautiful, Sydnee."

"'Beauty is as beauty does,'" she quoted her mother.

Brooks laughed and took a swig from his water bottle. "Oh? Guess you might be in trouble, then."

Her spine stiffened. She'd meant *him*. "I'm not the one who's full of himself and lies to people."

"I'll admit I'm confident, but I don't know what I've lied about."

She tried to think, but was coming up blank. "You ... you didn't tell me who you were when I met you the first time."

"Oh." He nodded as if that made sense. "The first time in the women's clothing shop, when you turned down my dinner invite and told me to come eat tortillas and beans at the orphanage?"

"Yes! That's it. As soon as I told you where I worked, you should've coughed up that you basically own me, ball and chain."

His eyes captured her gaze and wouldn't release her. "Please forgive me for owning you ball and chain."

Sydnee swallowed and bit at her cheek. She wanted to cross the distance between their chairs and sit on his lap like he'd suggested. Darn him and his come-hither glances. She didn't need this. "I don't think I can. Until you stop blackmailing, or bribing ..." She paused and thought. "Maybe it's extortion. I don't know! Whatever you're doing. But you didn't give me the choice whether to be here, so how can I forgive you for owning me?"

"Maybe together we can find a way," he suggested with an unnerving look that had her taking a long drink from her water bottle.

"Don't you need to watch where you're going?" She pointed out at the rolling waves and blue sky.

"The boat basically drives itself. We could go try out that master suite and be fine."

She clenched her teeth. "We are *not* trying out the master suite."

"Your loss."

"Why do you have to be such an overconfident jerk?"

Brooks smiled at her.

"I thought José would come with us to help you drive."

"And I thought you'd want to be alone with me." He winked and his hand rubbed along the steering wheel.

"Well, I don't." She got distracted watching his strong fingers on the wheel. She knew how those fingers felt on her flesh. Clearing her throat, she fished for something to say. "If you're driving by yourself, how will you sleep?"

"It's only four hours to Zack's island. I think I'll manage."

"So all that talk about the master suite? You were bluffing."

"Caught me." He grinned. "You want to learn how to captain the boat?" He issued the challenge in such a way that she had no choice but to accept.

"Love to."

He motioned to her. She walked on unsteady legs toward him. He took her hands in his and tugged her between his arms facing the steering wheel. Gently, he placed each of her hands on the wheel, keeping his hands over hers, and turned the wheel left and right a few times. She swayed, but stayed on her feet as the boat turned. His touch about drove her crazy. She couldn't concentrate on anything but the feel of his palms covering her hands.

"The throttle is to your right. Pretty simple: forward, back, and neutral. There's no brake, so you have to put it in reverse to slow down." He didn't release her hands, and though he stayed seated, he was much too close behind her. She could feel him and smell him. If she stepped left or right, she'd graze one of his muscular thighs.

"That's about all there is to it," he said.

"Don't be demeaning. I know there's a lot more to it than that."

"Not trying to demean, my love. It really is quite simple. The navigation takes a little more to ..."

Sydnee whirled to face him and his voice trailed off. She quickly realized her mistake as she was standing with his arms encircling her.

He licked his lips and studied hers. "Problem, love?"

"Yes." Sydnee should've broken through the circle of his muscular arms, run for the master suite, and locked herself in there for the duration of the trip. Instead, she swallowed and clamped her arms to her sides so she didn't reach up and touch his jaw. "You can't be calling me 'my love.'"

"I call lots of people love."

"Exactly! I am not one of your lovers."

His eyebrows quirked up.

"And you aren't supposed to be touching me. That's part of the deal."

"I'm not touching you."

She realized that was technically true. Though his arms were around her, they were holding the steering wheel. Yet if she tried to move she'd bump into his powerful arms, and the way he was looking at her ... she might as well have been hot woman on a stick. Okay, she could admit she liked the way he looked at her, but she wanted to be the only one he looked at like that, and the cold hard reality was ... that was a pipe dream with a man like Brooks.

Sydnee was getting fed up with his games. "Did you offer to teach me how to drive just so you could have an opportunity to put those brawny arms around me?"

Brooks smiled. "If I say yes, what will you do?"

"I'd say slap you, but that's a little too cliché."

"Thanks for sparing me that." He winked. "Why don't you just admit you want what I've got to offer, and we'll both have a much better weekend?"

Sydnee slammed her open palm against his chest, wincing at the sting in her palm and the jarring of her wrist. Brooks grasped her wrist between his fingers and gave her a little tug. The boat lurched to the right. Sydnee fell against his leg with a squeal like a trussed-up hog. Brooks wrapped his left arm around her and held her on his lap.

"Is that what you were trying to accomplish, love?"

She stared up into his handsome face, confused and wishing with everything in her that he was genuine. That she really could be his "love" someday.

"I think I'll go sit outside again," she panted out.

"You think? Does that mean you're sure you want to be outside, or do you want to stay right here?" His arm was wrapped securely around her waist, and it felt heavenly to be this close to him.

"Outside's probably safer."

Brook's eyes dipped to her lips. She caught a breath and waited. Would he try to kiss her? She wasn't sure how she was going to respond. His head lowered, and she was mesmerized by his dark eyes focused on her, like she was the only woman for him. But she wasn't. The instant before contact, she turned her head and his lips brushed her cheek. Even that much connection was too much. Shaking, and wishing she hadn't turned her head, she stood, pulling from his grip.

"I'll be out back if you need me."

"Oh, I'll need you." Brooks gave her a smile that kind of tore at her heart. Had she really made him that sad, or was he the best actor she'd ever met?

She fled for the back of the boat, forgetting her water bottle. She was thirstier for the man in the captain's chair than water, anyway.

CHAPTER ELEVEN

Zack was waiting for them when Brooks guided the boat into his friend's harbor northeast of Belize later that afternoon. Sydnee had spent the entire trip at the back of the boat. He vacillated between wanting to convince her he was the player she thought he was and wanting to pull her back onto his lap. He sighed. Trying to pull her back onto his lap would convince her he was a player, so maybe that *was* the route he should go. Why did she have so little trust in him and why couldn't he drop his pride?

He navigated the boat close to the dock and tossed Zack the lines. Zack secured them quickly. Brooks jumped off the boat and pulled his best friend into a manly back-slapping hug.

"My boy!" Brooks exclaimed. "I've missed you. How's the little family?"

"Good. They'll be excited to see you. Please say you brought presents." Zack rubbed his hand over his bald head. His dark eyes twinkled. "That's all Chalise has been talking about for the past week, the presents Uncle Brooks brings her."

"Don't worry. Uncle duties are at the top of my list."

Sydnee walked off of the gangway and Brooks took her hand to help her. She snatched it back quickly.

He sighed. This had been a horrifically bad idea. Instead of enjoying a weekend with his friends, he was going to be second-guessing himself with this woman. Would Maddie like Sydnee, or would that be awkward? This had the makings of misery. The first woman he took to meet his best friends, and he had probably chosen completely wrong.

Zack watched them both with a slightly open mouth. Brooks tried to think how to introduce her. "This is my ... friend, Sydnee."

"Employee, not friend," Sydnee said in a sickly sweet voice, making her ee's a long ā sound and thickening her accent. She stuck out her hand and Zack shook it. "It's nice to meet ya."

"Zack Tyndale," Zack said.

"I remember you from the Olympics."

Zack nodded. His skin was dark enough that he didn't blush, but Brooks knew it was embarrassing for him to think about his failed Olympics hopes. "Sadly, everyone does. Come meet my family."

"Family?" Sydnee asked, glaring at Brooks.

"What did you think I was bringing you to?" He licked his lips, elevating one eyebrow. He really did love to tease her.

"You know what I thought. Some ... singles party." She smacked his shoulder.

"I'm taking no responsibility for this one, love. They were your misinterpretations, not mine." Brooks held up his hands.

"Which you didn't try to correct." Her eyes were full of daggers.

"Something wrong?" Zack asked.

"Sydnee seemed to think I was bringing her to a crazy island kegger or ... something." He winked at her. No reason to spell out all her assumptions.

"Really?" Zack glanced over at Sydnee. "And you still came?"

Brooks would've laughed if Sydnee hadn't gone bright red. She'd accused him of being some womanizer, and with an innocent question, Zack made her look like a loose woman. Brooks almost thought it served her right, but then he felt guilty about her embarrassment.

"I didn't have any choice." The venom in her voice didn't give Zack anywhere to go with a follow-up question.

Okay, the guilt had disappeared, and yes, bringing Sydnee here with her defensive and uncomfortable attitude had been a rotten idea. They walked together up the stairs to the pool deck, Sydnee as far away from him as she could get.

"This island is amazing." Sydnee thankfully changed the subject. "Is it just you and your family that live here?"

"Yes. My wife, Maddie, and my three—"

"Uncle Brooks!" Chalise tore across the concrete with Izzy right on her heels. Maddie was behind them, lugging baby Alex. Maddie was an exotic mix of Italian and Spanish ancestry. Her adopted son was from Belize and looked enough like Zack that no one would guess he was adopted, but the little guy was almost as thick as he was long. Brooks might have to convince Zack to move back to the states at some point so Alex could play American football, or maybe rugby.

Brooks knelt down and caught Chalise in one arm and Izzy in the other. Standing, he spun circles as they shrieked with giggles.

"Where's our presents?" Chalise demanded when they stopped.

Brooks chuckled. Zack and Maddie were going to have their hands full with this girl. Izzy was quiet and unassuming, but Chalise made up for her more mellow sister which was a miracle on its own as she hadn't spoken for two years after her parents had been killed. Brooks related so well to Chalise, but his parents had left him willingly.

"Chalise," Maddie reprimanded softly. "Give Uncle Brooks a second to get settled; then I'm sure he'll find your presents."

Brooks set the girls down and Maddie gave him a hug. "Hello, beautiful," he said.

"Hey, you big lug." She transferred the baby to his arms.

Brooks recognized it was odd that he was so comfortable around these children but steered clear of the rest of the little people in the world. Yet he had no choice if he wanted to be with Zack and Maddie. These children had such a different situation than his remembrance of misery and anxiety—Chalise, Izzy, and Alex were loved and happy. The children Sydnee took care of had a hole in their hearts that would never be filled. The wishing for parents, for love, for acceptance. He understood every ache they were experiencing, and it scared him to death.

Shaking his head to clear it, he tossed the baby up into the air. Alex giggled. "He is a bruiser. Wow. How do you carry him around?"

Maddie laughed. "I can't stand to put him down. All that squishy body." She squeezed one of his chubby thighs, then inclined her head with a smile toward Sydnee. Brooks could just see the wheels turning in her head. "I'm Maddie Tyndale," she said.

"Sydnee Lee Swenson. It's nice to meet y'all. You have a lovely home."

"Thank you."

"I bet y'all enjoy lots of peace and quiet."

"We're very happy here, but it isn't too quiet with these monkeys around." She smiled affectionately at her children. "When Chalise and Isabelle start school in a couple of years we might have to go back to reality, but for now we'll enjoy paradise."

"Reality?" Zack pulled his wife close. "Managing my father's company via satellite and taking care of three kids and a beautiful wife is about all the reality I can handle."

She kissed him and laughed. "You love it and you know it."

"That I do." He bent and gave her a lingering kiss.

Brooks glanced over at Sydnee. She was studying him with a gleam in her eyes. He was going to hear some wrath about keeping the family a secret. Maybe if she didn't corner him alone, he could avoid being cussed out. Then again, he remembered the feel of her in his arms when he'd given her the brief piloting lesson on his yacht. A little wrath might be worth some alone time.

Brooks and Zack were play wrestling with the children in the living area while Maddie and Sydnee threw together a salad to go with the slow cooker dinner Maddie already had cooking. This was a side of Brooks she hadn't known existed. The family life looked good on him, really good. The little girls were head over heels for him, as she was certain most females could relate to, but the thing that was amazing was Brooks. She'd sensed at the orphanage that he didn't want to be around children, but these children seemed to bring him more true joy than she'd ever seen on his face.

"We're so excited that Brooks brought you with him," Maddie said. "We've been praying for a girl to capture him."

His friends wanted Brooks to settle down? Well, of course they would; married people wanted everyone to share their joy. Sydnee glanced discreetly at the men, wondering how much they could hear of the conversation. Would Zack tell his wife that Sydnee thought she was coming to a drunken party and she still came? Her Southern properness was chafing, and it was all Brooks's fault.

"You mean tricked me," she muttered.

"What?" Maddie's brow wrinkled. "Brooks has never had to coerce any woman. I think I'm the only woman that has ever turned him down."

Sydnee took a sidestep closer, still peeling a cucumber. This woman was a kindred spirit if she'd turned down Brooks. As gorgeous as Maddie was, she'd certainly turned down her fair share of men. Brooks having pursued her just reaffirmed what a flirt he was. "Tell me about that."

Maddie smiled. "I was already in love with Zack, or I'm sure I would've been tempted too."

These people were obviously part of the Brooks's fan club, but they seemed so normal and cute. Well, if ultra-wealthy, ex-Olympian who had been voted Most Beautiful Man in America turned husband and dad of three could be considered normal.

"He is pretty tempting," Sydnee admitted.

Maddie gave her a sympathetic glance. "Did he really trick you into coming here with him?"

Sydnee glanced up. Brooks had a little girl under each arm, but he wasn't twirling; he was looking straight at her. "He asked and I couldn't say no. How could anyone refuse Brooks?"

Brooks's grin lit up the room better than the floor-to-ceiling windows. He started bouncing with the girls as they laughed and laughed.

Sydnee half-wished she could confide in Maddie, but she didn't want to degrade Brooks in front of his friends.

"Like I said." Maddie smiled wistfully at her daughters in Brooks's arms. "I don't think there are many women that could turn him down."

Sydnee lowered her voice and stepped close enough that she rubbed Maddie's elbow. "Has he always been such a huge womanizer?"

"Well, he doesn't mean to … If only you knew him better." She shook her head. "Okay, yes."

"Do you ever think …" She couldn't believe she was asking this. "He would settle down?"

Maddie turned away and grabbed some salad dressings out of the fridge and put them on the counter. Sydnee snuck a glance at Brooks, but he seemed pretty busy, down on all fours, giving the girls horsey rides on his back. Oh my, he was cute like that.

"Sydnee and I are going to pick some mangos for dinner." Maddie grabbed her hand, and they hurried past the men and out one of the sets of French patio doors. Brooks caught her eye as she went past. There was a hunger in his gaze that gave her goose bumps. It was the kind of hunger she would worry about if they were alone, not sure if she could allow herself to reciprocate his obvious desire for her. It made her want to shout with joy and at the same time run and hide in her room.

Maddie closed the door behind them and led Sydnee past the pool around the side of the house to a fruit orchard and garden.

"Y'all don't live like a lot of rich people I know." She pointed to the garden. "Growing your own produce."

"I miss takeout, I'll admit it. But we're in New York one week a month, and we either eat out or let Zack's parent's chef cook for us. It's a nice break from cooking, but I like that our babies are getting healthy, homegrown food, and it's the perfect weather for growing lots of yummy produce."

"That is nice." Sydnee followed Maddie's lead, gently squeezing the mangos before plucking a ripe one. "So. Brooks?"

"You really like him." Maddie turned and faced her.

"I really don't know. Sometimes I like him, but mostly I want to hit him upside the head with a big stick."

Maddie laughed. "I think you're perfect for him."

"I wouldn't say that. I'm not impressed by his money or charm."

Okay, that was kind of a lie. His charm did draw her in quite well. "And I have a really hard time with a guy who has dated every attractive girl that crosses his path."

"I can understand that." Maddie brushed her long, dark hair over her shoulder. "I've been praying for the right girl to settle Brooks down. I know it's got to be hard to know there have been others before you, but he is honestly one of the best men I know. Besides Zack." She grinned happily. "But if you are the one for Brooks, I can promise you he would do anything in his power to make you happy."

"I just don't know if I can wrap my mind around all the women. He's like James Bond or something, giving you these looks, and who can help but swoon, right?"

Maddie grabbed one more mango, then started walking back toward the house. "I think most women would agree with you. Yet there are differences between him and James Bond."

"What differences?"

"Brooks is better-looking, a lot more fun, and he doesn't have sex with all the women."

Sydnee's jaw dropped. Maddie was blunt, but she appreciated hearing it from another source. "Are you sure?"

"Yes. When you get to know him better, maybe he'll share his conversion story. Then you won't have any doubt that I'm telling you the truth."

Sydnee followed her through the French doors. Brooks sat on the couch reading a princess book with a little girl on each thigh. Her heart melted a little too much. Especially when they all looked up at her, and he gave her that grin that would thaw an ice sculpture. Coming to this island may have been the biggest mistake of her life.

CHAPTER TWELVE

Thanksgiving morning dawned bright and sunny. Sydnee loved living in the Caribbean and never having to deal with winter and cold. After throwing the turkey in the oven and mixing up some rolls to rise, Maddie and Sydnee ate the delicious breakfast of scrambled eggs and sautéed veggies and papaya filled with cottage cheese and yogurt that Zack had prepared while Brooks entertained the children.

"I'd rather cook than wrestle with those three," Zack said, but Sydnee could see the love in his eyes. This family made her really miss home.

"Wanna go for a dive while we wait for that turkey to cook?" Brooks asked.

"I'd love to." Sydnee had only used scuba equipment a few times, but she'd really enjoyed the freedom of breathing and exploring underwater.

She went back to her room to change into her bathing suit. Eyeing herself in the bathroom mirrors, she really liked how this Nani swimwear fit. The black tankini top had a fun sheer lining above the chest and crisscrossed wide straps down low on the back. The high-waist floral bottoms were flattering and modest. She was glad her sister had found the online company and sent her several suits for her birthday.

She hoped Brooks would like the way she looked. Then she chastised herself for being shallow. It didn't matter what he thought. He was probably used to women who wore dental floss for swimwear. Sighing heavily, she searched through her suitcase, but couldn't find her cover-up. Should she throw on some shorts or forget it?

A hard rap on her door pulled her from the perusal of her suitcase. When she opened the door, Brooks was standing there in plaid swim trunks and a white T-shirt with his hand raised to knock again. His eyes went down her body and back up again. After several seconds, he closed his mouth and lowered his hand.

"I forgot to pack a cover-up." She folded her arms across the little bit of stomach the suit revealed.

"You don't hear me complaining. The suit is … very nice." He offered his arm. "Ready to see some fish, love?"

"If we must." She looped her fingers through his elbow and figured she couldn't call him out on using the word "love" all the time. He used it on Maddie and the girls almost as much as he said it to her. Besides, it was growing on her, or maybe he was growing on her.

He smiled. Zack, Maddie, and their children were already down at the beach. The little ones were happily digging in the sand. Zack walked with Brooks and Sydnee to the end of the dock, where the scuba gear was waiting. He handed Sydnee a snorkeling mask to try, and she tested it and then made a little adjustment. It was a lot higher quality than she'd used before, and it fit nicely.

"Have you done scuba?" Zack asked.

"I'm not certified, but I've gone out a few times on the island."

"Great. The nice thing about doing it here is that most of the reef is less than twenty feet deep, so you don't have to worry about diving or surfacing too quickly." He tapped her belt. "You just add weights to help you go deeper."

"Do I need to use those?" The weights and pressurizing always made her a little bit nervous.

"Don't worry. Brooks will stay with you and help you."

Sydnee turned to Brooks. He pumped his eyebrows. "We'll be buddies, love."

Why did he have to be so charming? "Have you brought other women here to scuba?"

Brooks' smile froze.

"I'm going to go play in the sand." Zack was obviously hiding a smirk as he walked back down the dock.

"Well, have you?" She needed this answer.

"I have to admit that you're my first." Brooks pulled off his shirt, and Sydnee forgot what they'd been talking about. What in the world would a person have to do to have muscles that sculpted? His chest muscles bulged, and there were striations on his arms and abs she didn't know existed before this heart-stopping moment. The silver cross hung between his pecs. Her mouth fell open, and she couldn't have looked away if an entire pod of dolphins had come to perform.

"You like?" Brooks pointed to his chest, flexing the muscles. They popped out even farther, and Sydnee barely stopped herself from reaching out to see what they would feel like under her fingertips.

She snapped her mouth shut. "You are *much* too confident."

"Confidence is simply a result of putting in the work and knowing you've got the stuff." He shrugged and lifted his hands innocently. Of course, that just displayed more impressive striations in his shoulders and arms.

She arched her eyebrows and tried to look unimpressed. It wasn't possible. "How much do you work out? I mean, honestly!" She gestured to his chest and blushed.

"A couple hours a day," Brooks admitted.

"Oh my." She gave a dreamy sigh, then immediately wished she'd controlled herself.

"Thank you for the compliment."

"I wasn't aware I gave a compliment."

"Your eyes said it all." He grinned. "Sit, please."

She sat on the edge of the dock, and Brooks lifted her right leg and ran his palm down her calf as he slipped a fin on. Sydnee decided she could have him touch her like that every day for the rest of her life and never tire of it. Brooks grinned up at her as he bent down and repeated the action on the left side. Sydnee was sad it was over so quick. He helped her get the heavy tank onto her back. His hands brushed her bare skin and sent her nerves into hyperdrive.

What had he said about bringing other girls? Something about her being the first. Really? "You've never brought any other girls here to meet Zack and Maddie?"

"No, ma'am."

"Why? The truth. None of your sass." Was he teasing her? Giving her the Southern answer with a fake accent to boot?

"I already told you the truth. I've never dated a woman longer than a week."

"Never?" Surely he was exaggerating.

He placed his hands on her shoulders and bent down to look in her eyes. "Never."

If he had tried to kiss her right then, she would have definitely given permission. She believed him, and her heart soared with the possibilities. He might've been a player, but maybe he had it in him to commit. To her.

Sadly, he released his grip and her gaze and proceeded to give her some instructions that she didn't pay any attention to. Brooks slipped all his equipment on, leaned backwards, and plunged off the dock into the water. Sydnee followed his example. The water was warm and wrapped around her body like a hug. She stood in the waist-deep water next to the dock, and Brooks did a few adjustments. She took her mask off, spit in it, and rubbed it around to help clear any fogging, then rinsed in the salt water.

"I think Zack already did the anti-fog spray," Brooks said.

"Oh." Sydnee's face flared. The anti-fog spray was expensive, so she'd never used it. "Great." She got her mask on, put her regulator in, and plunged her face into the water. Immediately she relaxed. Looking into the underwater world made her body feel weightless even with the air tank on her back. The ability to breathe underwater like a fish was magical. The water was shallow enough that all she saw was sand and a few small fish.

Brooks brushed against her and then took her hand. Sydnee kicked and swam with him. He took her around the dock, pointing out different fish that fluttered by. A sea turtle with a shell larger than a dinner plate swam past. Sydnee let out a happy squeal. Brooks took her away from the island to where the coral was thick, and tropical fish competed for space. He squeezed her hand. She looked at him, and he made the okay symbol with his other hand. She returned it. He tugged her deeper. Soon they were up close and personal with turquoise, yellow, orange, and pink striped fish. There were so many sizes and varieties, Sydnee couldn't identify them.

A black eel slid past on her right. Sydnee startled and screamed into her regulator. Bubbles burst out around her, and Brooks's eyes smiled at her.

They swam along holding hands. Sydnee loved being in this world that most people would never catch a glimpse of. Brooks' hand encasing hers was her safety net, and she liked knowing that he was there to protect her. Any worries about scuba, and being the one Brooks wanted to be with, dissipated like the bubbles from their oxygen tanks.

She had no clue how much time had passed when they swam back to the dock and then surfaced. The mask and oxygen tank suddenly seemed to weigh a hundred pounds. The warm air against her skin tickled as the water slid off of her.

"Pretty amazing, huh?" Brooks asked.

"I loved it. Thank you."

His grin showed those perfectly white teeth. "Glad to do anything that makes you happy, love."

Sydnee returned his smile. She was beginning to think that was the truth.

Thanksgiving dinner was better than any Thanksgiving Brooks could remember. The adults worked together to prepare everything, talking and laughing like old friends. The food was delicious. The children were entertaining. Brooks really did love these little ones. They were the only children he chose to associate with. He thought about what Sydnee did every day, all day: caring for children that weren't her own.

Could he do that? Giving money was easy. Could he step outside himself and really help? No. The memories of his childhood weren't scarred over enough to be around children who had no family.

Chalise, Izzy, and Alex were a different story. Yes, they were all adopted, but they were in the best spot possible now. This house was full of love and patience. It was what every child deserved. Brooks couldn't handle being around children who reminded him of his own childhood. He had to look tough, not like a wimp that was torn apart by the injustices of the world.

After dinner the little ones napped, and the adults played some card games, then watched a movie in Zack's theater. Zack and Maddie cuddled up on one of the sofas. Brooks was always jealous of their happiness, but today was worse than ever. Would Sydnee even want to sit with him? She was so different here on this island. She hadn't called him out or acted like he was going to attack her the entire day. It was like they'd called a truce. Was it temporary, or dare he hope this was their new normal? He grinned to himself. She'd been checking him out hardcore this morning on the dock. Not that he blamed her. He looked good, and he'd done his own share of checking her out. She was small in stature, but had a fit body and smooth, feminine curves that appealed to him immensely.

She settled into a love seat and he sat next to her. Glancing up at him, she gave him a soft smile that he hoped was an invitation. If not, he was going to make it one. Zack pushed some buttons and the lights dimmed. The movie started. One of the *Fast and the Furious* movies. He wasn't sure which. He didn't sit through movies very often, but he liked Dwayne whatever-his-name-was, the Rock. Kind of reminded him of himself.

He leaned closer to Sydnee. His arm brushed hers a few times; then he got brave enough to lift his arm and wrap it around her shoulder. She looked up at him, and then she leaned in. Brooks wanted to punch a fist in the air. He tugged her closer until she was resting against his chest. With a little sigh that had him dreaming of kissing her, she tucked her feet up on the couch and rested a hand on his abdomen.

Brooks thought this might be heaven. It had been a very long time since he had simply cuddled a woman. He couldn't even picture the face of the last date he'd wanted to just hold. He went on all kinds of fun or romantic dates; then he kissed them, dropped them off, and that was that. Not that he didn't want to kiss Sydnee, and soon, but he was really, really enjoying this holding her experience.

"The Rock is such a piece of work," Sydnee whispered.

"You think? I kind of like the guy."

Sydnee gazed up at him. "Reminds you of yourself?"

"What? Well, if you say so." He acted shocked, but was pleased she'd made the connection. But wait, she thought The Rock was a piece of work? What did that say about Brooks?

Sydnee lifted her hand and pressed it against his cheek. Brooks's breath caught in his throat.

"I guess I should like him, then," she whispered.

Brooks forgot they were watching a movie with Zack and Maddie on the next couch over. He wrapped both hands around her waist and easily lifted her onto his lap. Sydnee gasped, and it was such a cute sound. He lowered his head toward hers. He was finally going to taste those lips. She smelled like lemon candy again. Delicious.

"Uncle Brooks?" Izzy's little voice interrupted him like the needle being jerked from an old-style record player.

Brooks' head popped up. Sydnee slid off his lap, and he was upset with Izzy for the first time since he'd known the little girl.

"Yes, love?" He controlled his breathing.

"Can *I* sit on you?"

"Of course, my beauty." He lifted the child onto his lap, ignoring Zack's obnoxious laughter.

Sydnee was rigid beside him. Had he pushed too hard too fast? Today had been one of the best days he could remember in a long time. He hoped he hadn't ruined it with his desire to kiss her. He loved to kiss, but he was pretty certain kissing Sydnee was going to be better than even his imagination could conjure. A bit of terror raced through him. He usually pulled women in quickly and then just as quickly pushed them away. It was all about the fun of the catch.

Sydnee was a lot more work to reel in than anyone he knew, but the scary thing was, he wasn't ready to push her away, and he was afraid getting that kiss would just make him want more.

CHAPTER THIRTEEN

Though she missed being with her family in Alabama and her family in Cozumel, Sydnee had enjoyed every part of this Thanksgiving Day. Except how awkward she'd felt after Brooks had lifted her onto his lap and she'd almost kissed him with his friends sitting on the couch next to them. *My heavens.* Where had her brain gone?

They ate leftovers for dinner, and Sydnee forced herself not to be sad about missing Momma's sweet potato casserole or creamed potatoes. Zack's twice-baked potatoes were very good, and it was nice to try something different.

After dinner, she was changing back into her suit to swim with the kiddos when a knock came at her door. She hurried to answer it, smiling to see Brooks standing there.

He grinned at her and held out his cell phone. "I didn't know if you had coverage here and thought you might want to call your family."

She stared at him and had to blink away stinging tears. "Thank you. That was thoughtful of you."

He shrugged. "I'm just that kind of guy."

Sydnee laughed. He walked off to give her some privacy. She placed the call.

"Hello?" the beautiful soprano twanged out.

"Momma." Sydnee sighed, loving the feeling of home.

"Oh, sweet girl. It's Sydnee!" she yelled to the family. "You wouldn't believe who just dropped off a pie."

Sydnee didn't really care who'd dropped off a pie. She wanted to talk to her entire family at once and envision them sitting around the large farm table, their guts busting with yummy food.

"Jace," her mom continued. "That is one handsome young man, darlin', and filthy rich to boot. Your daddy might even give his approval of that one."

Sydnee rolled her eyes. Jace was a great guy, but he didn't make her tingle at his touch or dream of finally getting the opportunity to kiss him or laugh at his overconfidence. She talked with each of her family members, and Jace, for almost half an hour, then went looking for Brooks. He wasn't in his room, so she left the phone on a side table and found the family in the pool. Brooks waited for her in a lounge chair.

"How's the family?" Brooks asked, taking her hand and escorting her into the warm water.

"Everyone's happy and stuffed with pecan pie. Thank you."

"No problem." Brooks squeezed her hand.

It was so relaxing to just play with children and not feel responsible for them. Zack and Maddie were great parents, and Sydnee loved their adoption and wedding story. These children were very lucky to have them.

Zack and Brooks tossed the girls back and forth. Baby Alex was in his momma's arms, splashing the warm water and babbling. He reminded her of Tomás, and she felt a pang for her children. She knew they'd be fine without her, but she was anxious to hold Tomás and wrestle with Daniel and Alejandro. She should've called them too, but that would've left Brooks waiting for far too long.

Sydnee watched Brooks's arms flex as he threw Izzy to Zack, then snagged Chalise out of the air. Two hours a day in the gym? Yesterday she might have said that was excessive. Today she was pretty sure that was time well spent.

The sun set as they were getting out of the pool. Sydnee wrapped herself in a towel and watched the orange orb disappear into the ocean. "Y'all are so blessed," she said to Maddie.

Maddie cuddled her chubby son against her chest. "We are. Spoiled rotten."

"Spoiled with *love*," Chalise sang as she skipped past them into the house.

"Don't drip on that wood floor, little girl," Maddie called.

"I'll run fast, Momma." Chalise disappeared into the house with no towel, water streaming down her legs from her little swim skirt.

Maddie handed Sydnee the baby. "Would you take him while I go cuss my child?"

Sydnee laughed and gladly accepted Alex. It was kind of comforting that super wealthy, super nice people still had to discipline. Brooks came up behind her and leaned over her shoulder, playing a little game of peek-a-boo with Alex. Sydnee's breath caught at his nearness.

Alex shrieked with laughter and arched his back. Sydnee panicked and grasped him tighter, terrified this chubby baby would fling himself right out of her arms. Brooks' arms wrapped around both of them and pulled her back against his firm chest. She could feel the ridges of muscles against her bare back.

"I've got him, love."

"Looks like you've got us both." Her heart hammered in her chest. Brooks didn't release her, and Alex was oblivious to the way his uncle was touching this poor woman who could hardly handle any more intimacy. Alex babbled at them and blew spit bubbles.

"That would be a dream come true," Brooks whispered against her neck.

Trembling from his touch, Sydnee turned slightly and glanced up at him. He stared down at her, and every rational thought scattered.

"That looks good on you," Zack's voice came, as if from a tunnel.

"What?" Brooks murmured, not taking his eyes off of Sydnee's.

"The baby and the beautiful lady." Zack chuckled. "If you'll just excuse me, I'll take my son."

Sydnee snapped out of the trance, and Brooks released his hold on them. Zack lifted the little boy into his arms and tossed him gently. Alex laughed. It was a delightful sound, but Sydnee could only think of how many times Brooks had almost kissed her and they'd been interrupted. She should feel relieved. She wasn't sure if her heart or her nerves could handle being kissed by this man, but all she felt was repeated disappointment.

Zack had an undeniable smirk on his face as he ushered Izzy in front of him through the great room, and they disappeared.

Sydnee was alone with Brooks. The sky was streaked with pink clouds over the turquoise water, and a warm breeze lifted the hair off her shoulders. Sydnee was more than ready to see if his kiss was anywhere close to as exciting as his touch.

Brooks' hand circled her arm. Sydnee looked up at him. He took a step closer, and his strong body brushed against hers. His eyes were filled with desire for her and her breath shortened to small pants. Cupping her cheek with his palm, he slowly lowered his head. The waiting was agonizing. Sydnee pushed up onto tiptoes, needing to shorten this romantic moment or she was going to go insane with wanting him.

The French door banged open and Chalise barged out. "Will you help me find my mermaid Barbie, Uncle Brooks? I hasta have it in the tub!"

"Uncle Brooks is busy with something better than a mermaid," Brooks murmured as he stared at Sydnee. He released her, offering her a smile and a look that said he wanted that kiss as much as she did. The timing just wasn't right. Ever. "Let's go dive for it, love," he said to Chalise.

"Excuse me," Sydnee murmured, giving Brooks one last glance before she slipped into the house and to the bedroom they'd given her for the duration of her stay. She took a really long shower and then wrapped her hair up in a towel and wrapped another towel around her body. Surveying her face in the mirror, she liked the way she looked with sun-kissed cheeks and a glow in her eyes. What exactly was Brooks doing to her? His friends seemed to think this wasn't his usual mode of operation. She smiled at herself. She felt special to him.

A soft knock on her door brought her around. Oh, crap. She was in a towel. Rushing to the door, she opened it a crack. Brooks stood on the other side, grinning at her. "Can I come in?"

"No!" Sydnee slammed the door on him.

"Please, Sydnee. My yacht hit a water buffalo and I need your towel to wipe it up."

Sydnee laughed. "That was really lame."

"Can I come in *after* you get dressed?"

"I'll think about it," she shot back. Rushing to her suitcase, she pulled out underwear, a tank top, and some cotton shorts and hurried putting them on. She took the towel off her head and combed her fingers through her hair. A quick brush of her teeth and a spritz of her sheer cotton lemonade body splash was all she had time for. Her mother would be appalled at her lack of sprucing up.

Hurrying back to the door, she swung it wide. Brooks was still standing there. Yay for her. His dark hair was wet, and he hadn't shaved today. He was completely irresistible. Sydnee grabbed his T-shirt and tugged him into the room. "Get in here before Chalise interrupts us again."

Brooks pumped his eyebrows, coming willingly. "I like the way you're thinking."

"Well, don't get any ideas, big boy. I'm not letting you stay in here. I just need that kiss I keep getting denied."

"Wait a minute. I distinctly remember being told to not touch you on this trip. Hard to kiss you, love, if I can't touch you."

"You kiss me or I'll be hitting *you* with a water buffalo."

"So forceful." Brooks lifted a strand of wet hair off her shoulder and rubbed it between his fingers. "I like it."

Sydnee suddenly felt shy. Had she really just begged this man to kiss her? She glanced over his handsome face. Oh yes, she had, and oh yes, she was going to enjoy it. She pushed at his chest, backing him up into the door.

"Whoa." He lifted both hands palms up. "Somebody finally realized Brooks is the man she wants."

Sydnee couldn't help but laugh. He had no idea. She placed her hands on his shoulders and pulled herself onto tiptoes. "Maybe. We'll see if you can kiss with those beautiful lips as well as you can smart off with them."

"Better." Brooks wrapped his hands around her waist and pulled her against him.

He lowered his head and slowly, gently pressed his lips to hers. Tingles of pleasure and excitement raced from her lips and throughout her body. Sydnee ran her hands up his neck and explored the stubble on his face. Brooks moaned and increased the pressure of his kiss. He lifted her completely off her feet, turned a half circle, and pressed her into the door. Sydnee let out a gasp of surprise, but recovered quickly and wound her fingers through his hair. She inhaled the spiciness of his cologne and tasted warmth and peppermint. *Oh my, this kiss was worth waiting for.*

The door pounded behind her. "Sydnee?" Maddie called.

Brooks released her from the kiss and cradled her against his chest. Her feet were still dangling off the ground. He opened his mouth to respond. Sydnee clapped her hand over his lips and stifled a giggle. Maddie couldn't know he was in here. She loved this family, but their timing stunk.

"Yes?" Sydnee responded.

"We finally got the kids settled and Zack said his mango cheesecake has cured long enough. He's so ridiculous about waiting until the flavor has melded perfectly. He was going to find Brooks. Do you want to come have a slice?"

Maddie was talking forever and Sydnee was hung like a hamper here, but she was in Brooks's arms so she would never complain. "That sounds great. I'll, um, be right there."

Footsteps tapped away from the door. Brooks threw back his head and laughed. "Their timing is awful."

He set her feet on the floor, but then pinned her against the door and kissed her once, twice, a third time. Sydnee gasped for a breath. "Zack's going to have a hard time finding you," she murmured, trailing her fingers over his firm chest.

Brooks kissed her, then broke away and chuckled. "We're going to walk out there hand in hand and really give him a shock."

"If you stop kissing me now, I'm going to give you a shock."

Brooks grinned and proceeded to kiss her until Zack pounded on the door. "Brooks. If you're in there, Maddie is going to kill me."

Brooks roared with laughter. "I know you kissed Maddie in here plenty of times before you got married."

"Yeah, but I have more self-control than you."

Brooks leaned down to Sydnee's ear and whispered, "My woman's more irresistible than his."

"Only to you." Sydnee flushed, loving the thought of being his woman.

Brooks's eyes traveled over her face, and he nodded. "To me."

CHAPTER FOURTEEN

Friday morning, Sydnee slept late, and then she and Maddie swam laps in the pool while the men cooked breakfast and fed the children.

"I can't tell you how nice this is," Maddie confided in her as they stretched in the pool after they'd finished swimming. "I really needed a vacation."

Sydnee laughed. "Forgive me for saying this, but your life seems like a vacation."

"I guess it would." Maddie lay back into the water. "Don't let me complain, because I love my man and kiddos more than anything, but going from single graduate student to married with three children and isolated on an island was a bit of a shock. But we're figuring it out, and Zack is so good to me. He cooks most of the time and helps clean too." She chuckled. "This house was spotless before we got married."

"It's such a beautiful house and island."

"It is. I do love it here, and we get to do a lot of fun things with the girls."

Sydnee was surprised when she realized the moisture running down Maddie's face was not from the pool. "Everything okay?"

"Yes!" Maddie brushed the tears away. "Please don't think I'm not happy, because I am, I really am. I think I'm just hormonal. I'm only twelve weeks along and—"

Sydnee grabbed her new friend in a hug. "Y'all are pregnant?"

Maddie nodded and returned the hug. "Yes. I'm excited, but a little overwhelmed. Four under the age of four. Are we insane?"

"I think you're amazing." Sydnee felt such a pang of jealousy. She loved the children in the orphanage completely, but she also wanted what Maddie had someday. Her own home. Her own children.

Brooks poked his head out of the French doors. "Hey. That's my girl you're hugging, Madeline."

Sydnee grinned. Her own man. She wanted him first and foremost.

The two women broke apart. "You're not the only one who can hug her," Maddie retorted.

"I should be." Brooks winked. "Breakfast is ready, and since you aren't exercising anymore, Zack thought you might want to eat."

"Thanks. We'll be right in."

Sydnee smiled shyly at him. The kissing last night had been amazing. She hoped it would continue sometime today. She wouldn't complain if it was the main activity of the day.

Brooks gave her that grin that made her knees go to grits. Darn that man and his looks and his lips.

"Seems like you aren't bothered by him having dated other women anymore?" Maddie said as they climbed out of the pool and wrapped in towels.

"It sounds so selfish when you put it like that." Sydnee winced. "How can I blame a guy for something he did before I met him? It's just ... is he really going to give up a playboy lifestyle for me?" That was the main issue. She could realize those women were in the past, but what if she was just another conquest and as soon as he grew bored of her, he'd move on? How would she survive then?

"You'll never know if you don't give him the chance," Maddie said.

Sydnee pursed her lips and nodded. She'd never thought of it like that. It was a risk she had to take if she wanted to be with a man as fabulous as Brooks. He deserved that chance, and about a hundred more kisses.

They all went down to the beach after breakfast and alternated between digging in the sand and swimming in the ocean.

She and Brooks were laying on chairs side by side, their hands dangling and clasped together. She sighed and looked out over the turquoise ocean. Ideal, yet Maddie admitted her life wasn't perfect. Everyone had challenges no matter how fabulous or easy their life seemed.

Chalise and Izzy were digging and pouring sand into buckets while Maddie read a Jeanette Lewis novel. Sydnee loved the funky turquoise shoes the bride on the cover was wearing.

Now that Sydnee was paying attention, she could see a slight bulge on Maddie's lower abdomen. How exciting to be expecting their first baby. Well, not really their first, but their first together. She loved how Zack and Maddie showered love on their children, and except for their different coloring—Chalise's skin was much lighter than Izzy and Alex's—she wouldn't have guessed they were all adopted.

Zack had gone to lay the baby down for a nap, and everything was quiet and peaceful on the beach. Brooks squeezed Sydnee's hand and gave her a lazy smile. She looked over his fit body, and her mouth went dry. Would Maddie notice if she leaned over and gave him a quick kiss?

A scream of injustice ripped through the air.

Izzy blinked her eyes rapidly, digging her fists into them, and her screams turned to sobs.

"What happened?" Maddie jumped from her lounge chair.

"I no know." Chalise shrugged innocently, patting sand down and not looking at her sister.

"My eyes," Izzy wailed.

Maddie hurried to her younger daughter, pulled her hands away, and gently wiped at her eyes with a towel. Brooks grabbed a water bottle, picked up the little girl, and laid her on his lounge chair. He poured water over her eyes. "Try to open them, love."

Izzy cried harder at first, but as the sand was washed away, she calmed down. Brooks held her up, and she blinked, then smiled tremulously. "Thanks, Uncle Brooks."

"All better now, sweetie?"

"Yes." She wrapped her thin arms around his broad back and hugged him close.

Sydnee loved this tender moment. This was her favorite side of Brooks. Well, besides the kissing side.

"All right, little lady," Maddie said sternly, giving Chalise a stare down only mothers could give. "How did sister get sand in her eyes?"

Chalise shrugged and threw a guilty glance at Izzy.

"We've talked about throwing sand," Maddie said.

Chalise's lower lip trembled. "I sorry, Momma. I sorry, Izzy." A fat tear rolled down her cheek. "I didn't mean to."

Maddie sighed. "That's what you said the last twenty times. Come on. Let's go sit in time-out, then talk to Daddy." She stood and took Chalise's hand, leading her toward the stairs. She glanced back at them. "Are you okay with Izzy for a few minutes?"

"Of course," Brooks said.

Izzy seemed content to sit on the lounge in Brooks's arms. Not that Sydnee blamed her. He had that talent of drawing in women of every age.

"Thanks for coming a visit, Uncle Brooks." Izzy laid her head on his chest. "I love you."

Brooks held the little girl and glanced over at Sydnee. This wasn't his usual flirtatious or smoldering glance. She could swear she could see into his soul. This little family affected him. He did want this. He just didn't know it.

"I love you too, sweetheart," he said.

CHAPTER FIFTEEN

Brooks really enjoyed the relaxed day with his friends, and especially with Sydnee. He was pushing emotional boundaries here he hadn't consciously realized he'd established. He was sure a psychiatrist could diagnose him with some kind of commitment issue syndrome, and they'd probably be right, but he had thrived on the single life and his empty flirtations. Until she came along. He looked across the dinner table where Sydnee was feeding Alex baby food while Maddie talked Chalise into eating her salad.

Zack caught his eye and grinned. Brooks returned the smile, but his eyes strayed back to Sydnee. Her exterior beauty had initially drawn him in, but she was so much more than that. Was he? She was an American social worker who worked full time in a Mexican orphanage for a ridiculously low salary, and she didn't even speak fluent Spanish. How big of a heart did you have to have to do that?

He had this eerie feeling that when they got back to Cozumel, she would want him to come be with her at the orphanage, be with the children. He didn't think he could handle those interactions. Would he try it for her? She turned and smiled at him. Her big blue eyes twinkled happily, and those lips were begging him to sample them again.

Maybe he would try to get past his fears of seeing the emptiness in the children's eyes. For her.

After dinner, Brooks and Sydnee cleaned up while Zack and Maddie got the children to bed. It was so .... mainstream, and so comfortable rubbing shoulders with her in the kitchen. He had a lot of employees who took good care of him, but Brooks still knew how to work and he didn't mind doing dishes. If he did them with her.

The last pan was dried, and Brooks took Sydnee's hand. "Walk with me?"

"Sure."

They strolled out of the house, down the steps, and along the beautiful beach. The sun dropped down to the water, and Brooks stopped her when they were well away from the house. He tugged her against his chest and simply held her. She fit in his arms, her small frame completely encased.

She glanced up at him, and his gut tightened with apprehension. This beautiful spot. This beautiful woman. Is this how it happened to other men? They declared their devotion, and then they were lost? Was that even possible for him? An orphan? Unloved and deserted. How could he ever be worthy of someone as guileless and beautiful as Sydnee?

"Sydnee, I, you ..." Brooks closed his eyes and tried again. "I'm beginning to think. I mean, to feel." Wow. This wasn't him at all to be fumbling his words with a woman, but this wasn't just any woman.

Sydnee pressed her fingers to his lips. "Brooks. You're making a mess of this."

He gave a surprised laugh. "Yeah?"

"Yeah." She ran her fingers along his jawline, then tangled them in his hair. "It's okay. You don't have to do some big declaration or figure it all out. We might get back to reality and it might not be real, you know?"

Brooks sucked in a breath too quickly. Not real?

"But then again, maybe it will be." She shook her head. "Can we just slow it down and enjoy being together without trying to figure it all out right now?"

Brooks studied her. Was she scared? Or maybe ... she didn't want him like he wanted her. He wouldn't blame her. He was an emotional mess who'd been deserted as a child and had never committed to any woman. How dare he hope to start a relationship with a solid, good, and thoughtful person like Sydnee?

"Brooks." There was a warning note in her voice. She rubbed at the furrow between his brow. "Stop. You're worrying too much. It'll all work out."

Brooks wasn't so sure, but at least she was in his arms at this moment. He bent down and softly kissed her. "Are you sure?" He sounded like an uncertain wimp, but that's what he was deep inside, so maybe it was time to reveal that to someone.

Sydnee stood on tiptoes and pressed harder into him, kissing him until he almost forgot his insecurities. "No, but we can figure it out together."

Together? He really liked the sound of that. He lifted her off her feet, and she matched him kiss for kiss.

"Brooks!" Zack's voice came ringing from down the beach. "Maddie says to stop mac-daddying and come make her popcorn."

Brooks released Sydnee from the kiss and rested his forehead against hers. "Maddie loves my popcorn. Lots of butter." His breathing was so ragged he could hardly get the words out.

"Hmm." She ran her hands along his neck and had him tingling from head to toe. "I think this entire family just likes to interrupt when we're kissing."

Brooks chuckled. "Zack and Maddie probably owe me. The past year I've done my share of interrupting them."

"Well, let's give them something to interrupt." She stood on tiptoes and kissed him again.

CHAPTER SIXTEEN

The next day passed much too quickly. Sydnee hadn't realized how badly she'd needed a vacation or how horribly she craved Brooks's attention. She was like a woman who'd been denied chocolate and Diet Coke for years, and now she couldn't get enough. Unfortunately, or maybe fortunately, the little family persisted with their horrific timing and Sydnee and Brooks rarely had a moment alone.

She wasn't sure why she'd interrupted Brooks from whatever he was going to declare last night on the beach. What woman wouldn't want a man like Brooks sharing his heart? Yet she didn't know if either of them was ready for that. This weekend had been unreal. What if they got back to real life and things changed? Her heart wouldn't be able to take it, especially if he made promises and then chose not to fulfill them.

The little ones were struggling with naps on Saturday afternoon, so Zack loaded everyone in the speedboat, and they cruised out into the ocean. Brooks and Zack pulled out a parasail and took turns going up. The colorful sail looked beautiful against the blue sky, and they both seemed to have a lot of fun. Brooks' irresistible grin spread across his face as Zack slowed the boat and Brooks dipped into the water; then Zack slammed the throttle forward and Brooks soared upward again.

Sydnee realized Maddie probably wouldn't go up because she was pregnant. Sydnee had told the men to go first so she could "watch the experts perform," but now it was her turn. What now? She worried her lip between her teeth. Should she admit how terrified she was of heights?

Her stomach was in knots and her palms sweating as Brooks directed her toward the rear of the boat and started putting the harness on her. Even the touch of his warm palms couldn't distract her from the terror rushing through her.

He tightened the straps and smiled at her. "All set?"

"I'm terrified of heights," Sydnee spit out.

Brooks's eyebrows arched up. "Oh, love, you don't have to do this if you don't want to."

"She ready?" Zack called from the front of the boat.

"Shh," Maddie hushed him, cradling Alex and Izzy. Chalise sprawled across one of the front benches.

"Give us a second," Brooks said. He turned back to Sydnee and pivoted with her on the platform at the back of the boat so she was facing him and the open water and couldn't see Zack or Maddie. "I'm serious. No one is going to be offended if you don't go. Just say the word, and I'll unhook you and we'll have a pleasant boat ride through the ocean."

Sydnee took a couple of breaths. Her brothers would've teased her and forced her to try this, telling her she'd love it when she did. She probably would, but Brooks' understanding was so needed.

"Thank you!" She jumped into his arms. He caught her, but must've slipped on the wet deck. They toppled over into the water, the parachute falling on top of them. Sydnee gasped for air as the slick material covered their heads and pushed them under the water. She kicked madly with her legs and flailed her arms to get out from under the chute.

"What the—" she heard Zack exclaim.

The baby started crying.

Sydnee gasped for air but took in water. She started coughing, fear rushing in faster than the water.

Brooks pushed the parachute off of them and grabbed onto the platform, holding her out of the water. Zack grasped her hand and lifted her onto the deck with Brooks pushing from behind. She expelled the water from her lungs and immediately calmed down. Brooks easily lifted himself up, took one look at her, and started laughing.

"What was that all about?" Zack asked.

Sydnee joined in his laughter. The baby's cries quieted, but Izzy woke up and was watching them with wide eyes.

"I have no idea," Brooks said. He wrapped an arm around Sydnee's shoulder. "Next time you attack me, maybe don't do it with a parachute on your back."

"I can't control myself when you're near." Sydnee winked at him.

Brooks pumped his eyebrows. "I know, it's a problem."

Zack rolled his eyes and stomped away from them, picking up Izzy and carrying her to the captain's chair. "When you two stop your sickening flirting, are we going to put her up in the parasail or not?"

Brooks sobered and looked at Sydnee. She nodded.

"You sure?" he asked.

"Yes. I want to try it."

"Okay. It's really gentle. If you get scared, make the cut symbol." He drew his fingers across his neck. "We'll bring you in."

"Sounds good." She squeezed his arm. "Thank you."

Brooks nodded. "Anything for you, love."

Sydnee smiled. Brooks straightened the sail, and before she knew it, the boat was in motion, the sail caught air, and she was floating. She really did enjoy the sensation and assumed Brooks had said something to Zack, because they didn't take her up too high. It was a fun experience, but she was so caught up in thinking about how wonderful Brooks was, her mind didn't have time to experience much else.

CHAPTER SEVENTEEN

Sydnee didn't want to go home Sunday morning, but she missed all of her little ones. Maddie and the children waved from the dock as Zack tossed ropes to Brooks; then they were motoring away.

Sydnee sat in the chair next to the captain's seat. "It was a great weekend. Thank you, Brooks."

"I knew you couldn't resist the chance to be with me." He reached over and took her hand.

"I had such a choice. Jerk tricking me into thinking it was a crazy singles party."

"I may not have cleared up any misconceptions, but you came up with those assumptions on your own." He squeezed her hand. "Has your opinion changed about the charming and oh-so-good-looking Brooks Hoffman?"

Even though his words were his usual sarcasm, his voice was cautious and optimistic, making it easy to read between the lines. He was very different from what she'd assumed, and she was falling hard and fast for him.

"If I say yes, what are you going to do?"

"Show you these lips are good for more than just witty banter."

"You can't kiss and steer the boat." Her palms started sweating, and she bit her lip to hide a smile.

"Try me." Brooks winked at her and pulled her toward him.

Sydnee went willingly. Standing between his legs, she realized she was in the same spot she'd been on the trip down, but she felt vastly different now. She was no longer cautious around him. Far from it. She'd seen the real Brooks this weekend, and she felt like she couldn't get enough and hoped he felt the same.

He wrapped one arm around her waist and held on to the steering wheel with the other hand. Sydnee leaned down and brushed her lips over his.

"Glad to see you've finally become a Brooks fan." He took his other hand off the wheel and pulled her against his body.

"You have no idea." She kissed him hungrily, wondering if she could ever get enough of his touch. "What about steering the boat?" she panted out, much too affected by his touch.

"Are we far enough away that Zack won't worry?"

She glanced out the back of the boat. The island was a pinprick in the distance. "Yes."

Brooks jammed the boat into neutral. They drifted in the ocean as he captured her mouth with his, and she was soaring through a cloud of joy she'd never experienced.

It was quite a while later when Sydnee slid into the seat next to him, and Brooks put the boat back into gear. They rode in comfortable silence for a while, but Sydnee really wanted to know more about Brooks. The real Brooks.

"Will you tell me more about your adoptive father?" Sydnee asked as they cruised through the open ocean, blue stretching out on all sides.

Brooks smiled. "Mr. Hoffman was from England. Very prim and proper. Tea and crumpets and shields of honor and all that."

"You never called him Dad or by his first name?"

The smile slid away. "Never. He wasn't some warm and fuzzy father figure. He was my provider and my mentor. He saved my life, and then taught me all he knew."

"How did he save your life?" Wow. That was sad. She thought of her daddy, who complimented and hugged her often.

Brooks' forehead furrowed. "I lived on the streets of Oakland. Ran away from my third foster family when I was eight."

"At eight you were on the streets?" Sydnee blinked, hoping she'd heard him wrong.

He nodded tersely.

"What happened to your parents?"

His lips tightened. "I don't remember a dad. My mom deserted me when I was five. Dropped me off at kindergarten in the morning. Nobody came to pick me up at noon." He shrugged like it didn't matter, but it obviously did.

She squeezed his hand tighter. Her heart hurt for him. She could just picture a cute little Brooks with a backpack on, waiting at the school pickup with nobody coming. And waiting and waiting. Had the teachers hugged him, or had they just called the police and shipped him off to foster care? It brought tears to her eyes. "Oh, Brooks. I'm sorry."

He waved that away, and she didn't blame him. Her words were lame and empty, but what did you say to that? She had no clue how a mother could desert a five-year-old or how an eight-year-old could survive alone on the streets. At eight she'd been wrestling with her brothers and learning how to cook grits and being smothered with love by everyone around her.

"How did Mr. Hoffman find you?" she asked.

"I learned how to take care of myself, but I messed with the wrong group and got in a fight. A bad one. One of the kids had a knife and he ripped me apart. My friends didn't know what to do to help me. If we went to a hospital, they'd throw us back in foster care. Mr. Hoffman appeared like some stern schoolmaster. My friends disappeared and he took care of me. He always told me the Spirit directed him to me. He was a pretty spiritual guy." He fiddled with some dials.

"How old were you then?"

"Ten."

Two years on the streets. How did that affect someone? Mother deserted him. The only female figures in his childhood were his business partner and his cook. No wonder he'd flitted from woman to woman. She didn't want to think selfishly right now, but would he ever really settle down? If he hadn't dealt with all of this emotionally, he probably needed therapy above her pay grade.

He stared out at the endless ocean. "Mr. Hoffman took me to a hospital, and when they released me, he took me home with him. Not sure how he got around the foster care, but money does open doors."

"Was he wealthy?"

Brooks chuckled and said, "You could say that. Generations of family money as well as being one of the pioneers of hard money loans and private mortgage brokering. He took me to his mansion, and his assistant, Evelyn, and his housekeeper, Lou-Lou, spoiled and loved me. Mr. Hoffman did neither. He gave me his name, his fortune, a formal education, and all of his knowledge of weapons and fighting, but he didn't tell me he loved me until the day before he died."

That was heartbreaking, and she had no clue how to respond.

Brooks cleared his throat and continued. "He loved to fight, but he was very calculated and formal about it. One of his ancestors was a duke in England, but Mr. Hoffman's line came from a second son. Without the title, that ancestor went into battle; then all the men after that became warriors. It was a matter of family pride that was passed through generations. I think Mr. Hoffman was high up in the army in England when he was younger."

She liked that he seemed to feel that familial pride. Something to be a part of, even if it wasn't his blood relations. "What brought him to America?"

"His first wife was American, and she wanted to raise their son in America."

"He had a son?"

"Yeah. Died in Afghanistan. Special forces."

"How sad."

Brooks met her gaze. "So I was the replacement."

"Oh, Brooks, don't."

He shook his head. "It's okay. I'm grateful. He pulled me from poverty and a future life of crime, prison, or being stabbed to death."

She mulled that over for a few minutes. He did seem grateful, but everyone needed love, maybe even more than stability. She didn't know if she should say it, but she wanted to learn everything about this man. "So he made you his heir, but he never treated you like a son?"

"He did." Brooks gripped the steering wheel until his knuckles whitened. "He taught me everything he knew and loved me in his own way. I was just one of those needy kids who wanted more affection." He stared out at the expanse of water and muttered, "Pathetic, I know."

"Not pathetic at all." Heartbreaking was what it was. She was no therapist, but she thought he needed to get this out, and her dual degrees in child development and social work had taught her a few things. His love languages were obviously physical touch and words of affirmation, and it sounded like Mr. Hoffman had done neither. "Brooks? Do you think that's why you have gone through so many women? Looking for that love?"

Brooks turned to her, his eyes wide. "If I was looking for love, I'd go past the first date."

"You've dated so many." In her mind he was screaming for love and attention and obviously he got both from women, but he never let it go deep enough to form an attachment. Why her? Why now? "Maybe you weren't finding the right kind of relationship that could break through your barriers."

He smirked at her. "Is that social work lingo?"

"No," she tossed back. "It's caring about my man lingo."

"Oh?" His eyes swept over her, and he reached over and squeezed her hand. "Maybe I was just looking for the right woman who doesn't respect anyone's barriers."

She rolled her eyes.

"Hey, it's a theory worth exploring."

"What theory?"

"Me being your man theory."

"How are we going to explore it?" He just couldn't stay serious for very long, but she wanted him to be her man. Oh, how she wanted him.

"I guess we'll have to spend a lot more time together."

She bit at her lip. He was dodging the deeper relationship concerns, but giving it more time was probably the best route to take anyway, and more time with Brooks wasn't something she would complain about. "Sounds good to me."

CHAPTER EIGHTEEN

The next three and a half weeks fell into a familiar pattern that never lost the excitement. Every evening, after the children were settled, Brooks would come pick her up and they'd go get dinner, take a ride on his Harley, walk on the beach, or even just snuggle and watch a movie. Sydnee loved being with him, but each time she asked him to come earlier and spend time with the children, he had some excuse. It was confusing to her. How could he so obviously love Chalise, Izzy, and Alex, yet he wouldn't give her children a chance?

A few days before Christmas, Rosmerta came dancing into her room. "Mr. Hoffman brought his crew over. We all have the day off, and they're going to throw a fun party for the children all day. You should see the backyard. They're bringing in huge blow-up slides and everything."

Sydnee leapt off her bed. Brooks was going to be with the children? It was a Christmas miracle for her. She could already imagine the joy in Daniel and Alejandro's eyes as Brooks teased and wrestled with them. "Where is he?"

Rosmerta smirked. "Out front, begging me to go get you, please, please, please." She placed a hand over her heart. "How do you ever resist that man?"

"I don't."

Rosmerta giggled.

Sydnee quickly touched up her makeup and threw some jewelry on. Rosmerta and Camila could have the day off. She wanted to see Brooks interacting with her children.

"Have a fun day," Rosmerta called.

"You too." Sydnee practically skipped down the hallway and out the front door.

Brooks stood next to his Hummer in an untucked button-down shirt and jeans that clung to his muscular legs. "Wow," he said when he saw her. "I think this big guy needs some attention from the beautiful woman."

Sydnee laughed and hurried down the stairs and into his open arms, inhaling his spicy scent. "You're going to spend the day here?"

His brow furrowed. He kissed her quickly. "No. My friends are going to spoil your children all day. I think you need some quality Brooks time."

Her heart sank as the picture of him entertaining her boys popped. "But Brooks."

He shook his head. "Please, love. Just you and me. Please." His eyes were earnest and filled with that smolder that always lined her stomach with butterflies.

She wanted to make her arguments, but it wasn't the right time, and how could she possibly resist when he said please like that? She finally nodded. He grinned and pulled her in for a kiss. "You won't regret it."

"I know." Someday she'd have to find a way to help him past his issues and see if he could give these children a chance. He'd been so cute with Zack and Maddie's children, so she knew he had that characteristic of loving children in him. Brooks had her heart, but so did Daniel, Alejandro, Tomás, and all her kiddos. Could her two worlds intersect?

They spent the day just being together—scuba diving a drift dive along Palancar Reef. She'd never had a chance to do that particular dive before and loved all the tropical fish and turtles she saw. They even saw a small shark, which both terrified and thrilled her.

After diving, they went to lunch at the Lobster Shack. Brooks ordered the double lobster. Sydnee had no clue how he finished it, but it was fun watching him savor each bite. All those muscles must kick his metabolism into overdrive, because he could definitely eat.

They finished their lobster, paid the bill, and drove to a beach club. Brooks directed her inside with his usual confidence, his warm palm on her lower back. The greeter exuded happiness when she saw them: "Mr. Hoffman, Mr. Hoffman. Right this way, please, sir. So glad you come."

Sydnee should've been used to this. Everywhere they went on the island people gushed over Brooks, and he always got plenty of women staring longingly at him. Luckily, none had approached them yet. She didn't want to be the catty girlfriend.

The lady took them into the Islander Fish Spa and turned them over to the therapist there. The younger woman got them settled in a tank where little fish started nibbling at their feet. It felt like bubbles popping all over her feet. Sydnee giggled and tried to relax into the chair. Brooks squeezed her hand and laughed. "I've only done this once before, but it was kind of fun. I figured you never pamper yourself."

"Too busy."

He nodded. Sydnee appreciated him making this day possible and loved being with him, but she didn't know that she wanted this kind of life. She needed the purpose of being busy with the children all day. Brooks was busy managing investments, his businesses, and all his staff. She knew he did a lot of good things with his money, but his lifestyle still felt a little lacking to her, and she didn't know if that was something you told the man you were falling in love with.

He took her back to the orphanage after dinner and a walk on the beach. He hurried around to get her door and wrapped her up in his arms. Sydnee savored his tender kiss, then leaned her head against his chest and simply held on.

"I think I might love you a little bit, Sydnee Lee." Brooks kissed her forehead.

Sydnee sucked in a breath. Her lips trembled. "Just a little bit?" She glanced up at him.

His dark eyes sparkled at her. He framed her face with his hands.

"This is a big step for me, love. I've called so many women 'love' it doesn't have meaning to me anymore, but you—" He gently rubbed his thumbs along her jawline. "You are everything to me."

Sydnee's body warmed from his touch and the searing look in his eyes. For better or worse, he made her believe that he meant what he said to her. But, was he ready to commit to her *and* her life with the children? They'd soared past his commitment issues, and now she wanted to push him to another level that would probably be much more uncomfortable for him.

He lowered his head and kissed her until she wasn't sure which way was up, but she was sure that she never wanted to let him go.

Finally coming back to reality, she sighed and smiled at him. "You make me very happy, Brooks Hoffman. I don't have to think about it. I do love you."

His grin was of the caliber women wrote poetry about. He kissed her again, the passion and love swirling around them. Sydnee loved being with him, especially when she was in his arms. He released her lips and whispered, "I'd better let you get inside."

"Come with me," she begged. "Your staff is all here, and the children are probably settled into bed. I always sing to them at night. You don't have to do anything, just be with me." She hoped this would be the path to melding her two worlds, taking it slow and easy with Brooks getting to know her children and seeing how happy and darling they were.

Brooks shook his head quickly. "No. I can't."

"Can't or won't?" Sydnee's stomach dropped. Why did he fight this so hard? She couldn't really comprehend his upbringing, but somehow they had to get past it.

Brooks' arms dropped away from her, and she shivered even though it was over seventy degrees. "Please don't push this, love. I can't. It's too hard."

"Brooks. You say you love me, but this is part of me. I need you to do it with me. I need you to love these children with me."

He backed a step away. "No. Can't we just be ... us?"

"But part of me is the children. You would love them; just give them a chance."

"I am giving them a chance. I'm providing for them financially."

Sydnee didn't say anything. He was right. Why couldn't she just leave it at that? Because she wanted to be with him in every part of her life, and she really didn't understand his obvious discomfort. Why was this so hard for him?

He shoved a hand through his hair. "You don't know what you're asking, Sydnee. Isn't it enough that I've committed myself to you?"

Sydnee wanted to say yes, this was a huge step for him, but didn't he see how much she loved these little ones? If she was a single mother, she knew he would give *her* child a chance. "Brooks, I've fallen in love with you, but I need all of you. Can't you give me that?"

"If you loved me, you'd understand why I can't."

"How do I understand when you won't even try? At some point you have to let go of the past and live your life." Maybe he had been too damaged as a child. How could she help him through that? She knew her children must remind him of pain from his childhood, of his lack of a stable family, but there had to be a way to get past that.

He studied her for so long she knew his answer wasn't going to be good. "You don't want me to live *my* life; you want me to live yours. I can't be with these children, Sydnee. I can't."

A taxi rolled up to the front of the orphanage. Brooks stepped in front of Sydnee. She appreciated his automatic protection. They didn't get a lot of visitors, especially at night and arriving in a taxi. The door opened, and Sydnee peeked around Brooks's shoulder.

"Hey, y'all." The voice and face were a shock. "Can you tell me if Sydnee Lee is here?"

"Jace," she whispered. It was him—tall, easy smile with the sandy blond hair and ocean-blue eyes that were as familiar as her own siblings. What was he doing here?

Brooks turned and gazed down at Sydnee. Their eyes connected, but she didn't know what message she was sending. Would he think she'd invited her old boyfriend to come visit? Of course Jace would appear when they were fighting instead of kissing.

Brooks stepped back and muttered, "Here she is."

Jace gave a hoot and jogged across the driveway. He picked her up, swinging her around and laughing. "Sydnee Lee! You look and smell as good as Momma's lemon cream pie."

Sydnee forced a laugh, getting dizzy from the swinging. Jace smacked a kiss on her lips, then finally set her on the ground. She looked around desperately for Brooks. The roar of an engine told her everything she'd feared. He pulled slowly away. She wanted to chase after him. Things were a mess between them, but she didn't know how to make it right. He couldn't see her point of view, and she was struggling to even want to see his.

Jace beamed down at her. "How've you been?"

Sydnee forced a smile. "It's kind of a bad time, Jace."

"Bad time? I thought this would be the best Christmas present I could give myself." He winked at her.

"I'm dating someone," she blurted out.

"That big guy?" Jace pointed where the Hummer used to be. "Seems to me a Southern girl would date somebody with a little better manners."

"Oh, Jace. You have no idea what you're saying." Brooks's manners were impeccable. It was his elephant of a past that was going to ruin their chance at happiness.

He slung his arm around her shoulder. "You got time to sit on the porch swing and tell me about it?"

Sydnee looked up at him, tears coming to her eyes. They'd been friends for a long time, and she could really use somebody to talk to. Maybe Jace coming was a good Christmas present for her as well.

CHAPTER NINETEEN

The next two days dragged by with Brooks trying to distract himself with work, exercise, riding his Harley, or taking his jet boat out for rides. Nothing worked, because nothing mattered to him anymore except Sydnee, and she was probably with that preppy guy with the Southern accent. Even if her old boyfriend hadn't shown up, she was still a do-gooder who'd adopted an entire houseful of orphans as if they were her own. He wasn't ready to be in love with somebody like that. Just the thought of seeing the pain in those children's eyes brought all of it back to him. The beatings. The hunger. The feeling of no one really caring if you lived or died.

Could he let go of his past and give those children a chance? What if that was his only path to being with Sydnee? He loved her, but he didn't know how to reconcile what she wanted and what he could handle.

Christmas Eve was miserable. He'd given his entire staff two days off, and he hated being alone. He only wanted Sydnee for Christmas, and he couldn't have her. Mr. Hoffman had always told him that when he was feeling miserable, he should help somebody else. He finally forced himself to call Camila and wrote down two pages of info, went into town, and bought toys, clothes, treats, anything he could see that the children might like. Several women hit on him, cooing about him buying children's toys. He gave them an empty smile and walked away. Sydnee had ruined him.

Even though he didn't know if they'd ever reconcile, he couldn't resist buying gifts for Sydnee. In a jewelry store, he saw a diamond ring that drew him in. He'd never bought a ring for a woman. Was it time to change that? Could he change other things also?

He waited until nine p.m. to go to the orphanage. If the children were already asleep, Sydnee couldn't ask that he visit with them. He really hoped that Jace guy had been sent packing. Was it too much to ask for more time? Time to deal with his past and his insecurities. What if seeing these children brought back all the loneliness and fear? What could he really do to help them have the love he'd never had?

He unloaded bag after bag onto the porch, not sure if he should text and see if she'd come out and talk to him or if he should just leave it alone.

The door opened behind him. "Wow. Somebody likes to spend their wads of money."

Brooks whirled around, and there she was, leaning against the doorframe in a tank top and yoga pants. Her hair was pulled back in a ponytail, revealing her slender neck. The air sucked out of him. She was beautiful, and he'd missed her more than he could ever express.

"They're, um, for the children." He'd left Sydnee's gifts at home, not sure when or if he would give them to her.

She nodded. "It's very thoughtful of you."

It was too stiff, too awkward. He couldn't even hear her accent. "Where's Jace?" he blurted out.

"Back in Alabama, I assume."

His heart leapt at this news. She had sent the old boyfriend packing, but what if he came back? Brooks had never been so uncertain about where he stood with a woman in his life. He pushed a hand through his hair, not sure where to go from here. How to win her back, or if he even could do that emotionally right now? Was it too much to ask that she just love him? Was he really back to his childhood, where love and survival were conditional on toeing the line?

"Do you want me to put them somewhere?" He gestured to the gifts.

"Sure. Let's take them into the gathering room. Rosmerta and I will wrap them tonight. Thank you."

He simply nodded, grabbed a pile of bags, and followed her inside. It took them far too little time to deposit everything on the tables.

"I asked Camila," he said. "She gave me a list of what they wanted or needed. I bought a few extra things too."

Sydnee reached out her hand, her blue eyes soft and welcoming. "It's a great gesture, Brooks. Thank you."

He engulfed her fingers between his much larger ones and got brave enough to ask, "But is it enough?"

She looked down. "I've missed you so much."

"I've missed you too," Brooks admitted, his voice husky and uncertain.

"Will you stay? Say hi to the children?" The begging in her blue eyes tugged at him. How could he resist her?

Brooks shook his head. Why did it have to come back to this? He tried to extend a branch, and she wanted the entire forest. "No. I can't, Sydnee." *Not yet.* Maybe someday. Who knew what day. Would it be soon enough for her?

"Oh, Brooks." Her shoulders rounded. "How can I help you get past this? What are you afraid of?"

"I'm not afraid." He puffed out his chest and tried to look threatening. Him, afraid? He hadn't been afraid since the night Mr. Hoffman pulled a knife out of him and taught him how to fight.

"You are. Why?"

She stepped closer, her eyes filled with a challenge, but also with too much sympathy. He wanted her to adore him, not feel bad for him. Brooks *was* afraid. Afraid of disappointing her; of losing her. He held his ground, barely.

"Talk to me. Please. Tell me why you can't come say hi to them."

He cleared his throat and waved an arm at the piles of presents. "Most women would be thrilled with the huge amounts of money I donate."

"I'm not most women, and while I appreciate all you do, this isn't about the money," she said. "They need love and attention too."

"Well, um, that's what you're doing for them."

"I don't have enough time and energy for eighteen children. Oh, Brooks." Her big blue eyes pled with him, and her voice was so earnest and kind. "You do so much for them already. Can't you please take that next step and come wrestle with Alejandro, kick a soccer ball with Daniel, or hold baby Tomás?"

His head shook violently. A baby. An innocent baby with no parents to love him. *No.* "I've got to go." But he didn't move.

She stepped closer still, and Brooks involuntarily stepped back. "Please," she murmured, and walked forward again. Brooks retreated until his back was against the wall.

"You can do this, Brooks," she said louder, and placed her hand on his chest.

Brooks grabbed her hand, getting a little angry. What right did she have to demand this of him? Tell him he could "do this" like some peppy cheerleader. Nobody but Zack and Mr. Hoffman knew about his secrets and insecurities. He'd told them a lot of it, but only those who had been there could really understand the ache in your stomach when you didn't know where your next meal was coming from. The constant fear of wondering who might beat you up next just because there was no one there to defend you and they liked to hear you scream.

He wished he could explain it to Sydnee, but she came from love and would never be able to understand. She could sympathize, but he didn't need that. He needed her to realize that he wasn't that guy who loved and helped children who had no one.

After more than twenty years, the agony of being deserted by the woman who should've loved him was still too painful. He'd waited hours on the school steps while the secretary and principal tried to find someone who wanted him. The secretary had given him some bubble gum. He'd slowly chewed it as he watched all the other children's parents pick them up. The too-sweet bubble gum flavor had mixed with the tears he'd tried to swallow. His throat felt thick and sticky, and his stomach hurt just thinking about it. Even the scent of bubble gum could make him nauseated.

Finally, the police came and took him to his first foster home. The first of several that seemed to only want children for the government money. He didn't understand why they were so distant and unattached. He assumed his foster parents didn't want to deal with him, because who would want a kid whose own mother didn't even care if he lived or died?

The children at Bethel had no one. He knew Sydnee, Rosmerta, and Camila tried, but it could never be the same as a whole family. Parents who thought their child was the best thing in the world and siblings who would be there for a brother. It would break him to see the sadness he'd lived with for an eternity, before Mr. Hoffman came along, etched into their innocent faces.

Sydnee's blue eyes were full of challenge and yearning, but he wasn't going to back down to a pint-sized blonde no matter how much he wanted her and—yes, he could admit it—he loved her.

"That's enough," he ground out. "I'm not scared of you or a bunch of children."

"Scared?" Her eyebrows arched up. "I didn't say you were scared of me."

He held her hand in his and marveled at how small it was. It had only been a week and he'd missed every part of her. "Then why are you backing me into a wall, trying to intimidate me?"

She gave a sad little laugh at that and placed her other hand on his chest. "You're twice my size. How could I intimidate you?"

"You're pushy and you *never* take no for an answer. That's as intimidating as ... anything."

Her mouth screwed up in frustration. Brooks got temporarily distracted by how cute she was. He was sure the children adored her just like he did.

"I'm just trying to help the children ... and you."

"Well, forget about trying to help me. I'm fine. More than fine. I'm a billionaire playboy and I can do anything I want to do." Better to put up his shield rather than have her see him for the wimp he was. So what if he'd dated every attractive woman on the island and had no desire to contact any of them again? How was he going to say goodbye to Sydnee when she was all he wanted?

"I thought you wanted more. I thought you wanted me," She whispered it, but the words penetrated to his soul, and Brooks couldn't look away from her blue gaze.

He wanted more. He wanted all of her, but he wanted more too. He released her hand and stood there, stunned.

She raised herself up on her toes, leaning closer. "Let me help you, Brooks. Please, let me in."

"How?" His breathing was ragged as he looked down at her. She was a beautiful woman, and he'd been drawn to her for her looks initially. But, she had more substance than just looks, and for the first time in a long time, he wanted someone to help him.

"Let me in," she whispered and gently tapped near his heart. "In here."

Brooks blinked at her and swallowed. She was so appealing, staring up at him with those big blue eyes and those soft lips. Before he could stop himself, he'd wrapped both of his hands around hers where they rested on his chest, bent down, and tasted her lips. She jerked in surprise, but then she pressed herself against him; he wrapped his arms around her waist and they fell into sync. Her lips tasted like cinnamon and were soft and moldable. She smelled just like he remembered— lemon cake or candy, sweet and intoxicating. He loved her far too much.

She drew back too soon, her breathing as ragged as his. "I love you, Brooks. Please let me help you."

He released her. "I'm not ready." Why didn't he just tell her he loved her and get this obsession she had of him interacting with the children over with? It couldn't be as bad as he feared. But then again, maybe it could.

"Will you ever be?" she whispered.

Brooks closed his eyes rather than face the disappointment in her gaze. He didn't know the answer to her question.

"That's what I'm afraid of." She walked backward two steps, her eyes fastened on his face. He had nothing to give her. He didn't put up a hand, walk toward her, or ask her to stop.

Her lip trembled, and she took a long breath, then whirled from him and rushed out of the room. He sat there, trying to catch his breath.

"Guess she didn't want to help after all," he muttered to himself, and slipped out of the building before he saw Sydnee again—or worse, any of the children.

CHAPTER TWENTY

Sydnee, Rosmerta, and Camila wrapped presents until early morning, resorting to newspaper when they ran out of gift wrap around one a.m. Sydnee sniffled back tears the entire time. Her friends asked her a few times what was wrong. She'd just point to the presents, mutter, "Brooks," and go back to wrapping. They finally stopped trying to draw it out of her.

How could he be so generous with his money? He'd spent the time to buy all these presents, and that image melted her heart. She wished he would try to interact with the children. He knew how much they meant to her and how much he meant to her. Was she ever going to find a compromise between her two loves? Right now it seemed impossible.

She gave a big sigh, stacking another present on the pile. The children were going to be thrilled tomorrow morning, and it was all due to Brooks. She needed to stop trying to change him and think about what she could change about herself. Did he just need more time? Maybe he'd be willing to meet with a therapist and talk through his past. Maybe she needed to let go of these children and just love Brooks. Her heart broke thinking about losing him or them. Patience definitely wasn't her strong suit, but she'd wait for him. She'd do about anything for him.

She finally climbed into bed after a tearful prayer. Tomorrow was Christmas, and she was going to make it fabulous for the children. Well, Brooks' presents would make that job pretty easy. First break she got, she'd go to him, tell him how much she loved him and how she wanted to understand and be there for him. But what if his childhood trauma was so great he could never make these children a part of his life? Could she say goodbye to them? Daniel's grin when he scored a goal flashed through her mind. Baby Tomás wrapping his chubby fingers around hers as she fed him a bottle. Darling María and Ella skipping around the yard, holding hands and singing.

She heard a movement next to her bed. "Alejandro?" she whispered. He was her most common nighttime visitor. Usually a song and a prayer and she'd have him back to sleep.

A hand clamped over her mouth and a smelly body came down hard on hers, pinning her to the bed. Sydnee grabbed at the hand, trying to pry it away as she squirmed to free herself.

"Don't fight me," the man whispered harshly in her ear. Cold steel pressed against her bare throat.

Sydnee whimpered. Was he going to rape her in her own bed? Long seconds passed, with Sydnee praying for some way to avoid what was coming and the man's ragged breath assaulting her cheek.

He moved the knife and she caught a full breath. He jerked her to her feet, pulling her against him. A rag was shoved in her mouth. It tasted like dirt and gasoline. The man wrapped it around the back of her head and tied it. She dry-heaved, but luckily didn't vomit. He tied her hands behind her back. It was too dark to see her captor, but she thought his voice and smell were familiar. Her body felt like lead as he dragged her down the hallway. The nightlight illuminated the hallway, and she could see several other men dragging children out the back door.

Brooks had paid to install an alarm after the boys had been taken last time. Why hadn't it gone off? Were these the same traffickers or somebody else? She craned her neck to see the man holding her, and cold sweat appeared on her brow.

"Remember me?" he taunted quietly.

Sydnee whipped back around. Had the police released him, or had he escaped? It didn't matter now; the man who Brooks had saved her from weeks ago was back, and no one was around to rescue them.

Brooks couldn't sleep. All he could see was Sydnee's beautiful face as she begged him to give the children a chance, and he said no, slipping back into his playboy mold who didn't need anyone. How could he say goodbye to her? Why, when he had finally fallen in love, did it have to be with a woman who wanted him to change, to be some benevolent uncle to all these neglected children who would only open wounds he could never deal with?

He rolled over and punched his pillow. He missed her. He missed her so much it hurt more than it should have. Like his mom had deserted him all over again. He was a mess. With all his stinking money, maybe he should hire a psychiatrist or something. Someone had to be able to fix his twisted mind.

Sydnee. She could fix it. But how many chances was she going to give him, and could he really make the effort with the children? He might not be able to change, but he was tough and he would try. Tomorrow. His first Christmas present to her. He'd go and visit and he'd wrestle with Daniel and he'd hold a baby if that's what it took, and if it freaked him out, he'd find the best psychiatrist he could, and he'd work through issues he'd buried for years.

His phone vibrated on the nightstand. The orphanage's number. Sydnee? His heart leapt. She hadn't been able to sleep either. Dare he hope she would give him a chance to fix things?

"Hey." His voice was all husky and needy. He needed her more than he could ever express.

"Mr. Hoffman! Sydnee! Los niños!" Camila started speaking so rapidly in Spanish he realized he wasn't as fluent as he thought he was.

"Whoa, whoa, calm down. What happened to Sydnee and the children?"

"Se los llevaron! Men in a truck. They're gone!" She wailed and cried and kept rattling on in Spanish.

Brooks sprang from his bed, throwing clothes on and hurrying for his weapons room. The traffickers. José had worried they might get released by the local police before they were transferred to the mainland for trial. But Brooks had paid to have security installed. He should've done more. Should've hired guards.

Sydnee. Not Sydnee!

He had to hang up on Camila so he could call José. He explained the situation as quickly as he could.

"What do you need?" his friend asked.

Brooks liked to fight alone, but this wasn't just a fight. It was Sydnee and her children. He knew she loved them, probably more than she loved him. "I need information. Find out where the traffickers would take them. And I need ... help."

"All you had to do was ask. I'll meet you at the yacht club."

"Will they take them to the mainland?"

"Not if they think someone might be coming for them. If it's the same guys as before, I'm betting on Guatemala."

What if it's not the same guys? Brooks didn't dare ask. He did the only thing he could—hung up and started compiling weapons.

CHAPTER TWENTY-ONE

S ydnee and four of her kids were in a small bedroom of an older yacht. Sydnee had overheard crying and talking from the rooms on both sides of theirs. How sickening that there were others being taken from their homes, too. Possibly others from her own orphanage. She'd been in a truck with only these four.

Sydnee lay on the bed with María on her lap and Alejandro under one arm. Daniel paced the small space between the bed and the wall, bouncing a whimpering Tomás. At least the traffickers had pulled off their filthy gags and untied them. Honestly, that scared her more than if they'd been left bound and gagged. The traffickers knew they had no hope of escape. If she was alone she might jump overboard given the chance, but with the children ... she was helpless.

"Let me take him from you," Sydnee said.

Daniel shook his head and gestured to the children in her arms. "No. You wake them."

Sydnee sighed and leaned her head against the wall. Daniel was mature beyond his years. He might learn more horrors than either of them could imagine in the next little while. She thought of Brooks again. He'd been through terror like this. Possibly in a worse situation at an age even younger than Daniel.

She'd been so wrong to push him to get over his past when she had no clue how it felt to be scared, alone, and knowing that pain, hunger, and terror were coming. At least these children had her. Brooks had had no one. She wished she could sit and hold him and he could share with her the memories, the fears, and the pain. She wished she could take it all away from him.

She pulled María and Alejandro in tighter, blinking to keep tears at bay and praying the same broken prayer over and over again: "Please send help. Please send Brooks."

Brooks, light, and happiness seemed so far away. Would she ever see him again? If she did, she'd beg his forgiveness, and she would never make him change. They'd work out some kind of compromise. She'd go help at the orphanage for a few hours each day, and then she'd give every other minute to Brooks. If he ever overcame his fears of being with the children, that would be heavenly, but she'd never force him to that. She could only pray that he'd give her the chance to explain how wrong she'd been and forgive her.

She let out a soft moan as she looked around at the four walls enclosing them. Would she even get that chance to apologize to Brooks? If she never escaped or died, she could only pray that he wouldn't let her misguided attempts at reconciling him with the children make him feel even more worthless. She prayed he'd find love and happiness that didn't put demands on him. She loved him so much, and she'd messed everything up. What she wouldn't give to make it right.

Brooks stood at the helm of his yacht. They were approaching the third ship of the night. The other two had turned out to be clean. He should feel guilty about waking honest people in the middle of the night, but he could only think of Sydnee. He'd heard all the horror stories of traffickers' treatment of prisoners and especially women. He couldn't stand the thought of someone hurting Sydnee, especially ...

He growled and focused on pulling as close to the boat as he could.

If they didn't stop, he'd have to ram them and hope he could leap onto their decks.

José held the bullhorn to his lips and barked out, "U.S. Coast Guard. Slow your speed and prepare to be boarded." It had worked well with the other boats, his accent masked by the sheer volume of the bullhorn. Even in international waters, sailors still feared the Coast Guard and usually complied with their wishes, no matter if they had jurisdiction or not. Brooks got the idea from when he, Zack, and Maddie had been stopped last summer by the Coast Guard in the middle of the night. He'd obeyed, even though it had about killed him to submit and not be the man in charge.

The boat slowed and then stopped, and Brooks heaved a sigh of relief, yet he wondered if their compliance meant they weren't the traffickers. He grabbed his M249, his favorite light machine gun. His knife and 1911 pistol were already on his belt.

"Be safe," he muttered to José as he and the other men boarded the boat. There were only a few men on the deck of the outdated yacht, covered with peeling paint and rust spots. One of them started talking to José in rapid Spanish. Brooks only caught part of it, something about them having no right.

"Give him Sydnee's description," Brooks instructed.

José did, and the man's eyes widened. Another man walked up the stairs. Brooks recognized him. The loser who'd kidnapped Sydnee several weeks ago. He *had* been released. Brooks saw the first man going for his gun and didn't waste any time.

"Down!" he shouted to his men as he lifted his machine gun and shot the man reaching for his gun in the shoulder. The man screamed and dropped his weapon. Another gun glinted in the overhead light. Brooks sprayed the man with bullets. Mr. Hoffman had always taught him to only kill when necessary. Tonight it might be necessary. The third man who'd originally been on deck was tackled by José. He didn't put up much of a fight. Disappointing. Brooks was ready to thump someone.

Brooks looked around. The trafficker he'd recognized had disappeared back down the stairs.

"Secure the boat," he instructed his men, running for the stairs and pumping down them. He might be running straight into a bullet, but Sydnee was down here. He could feel it. He would take that bullet if it meant saving her.

CHAPTER TWENTY-TWO

Sydnee heard the call from the Coast Guard and felt the boat slow. The Coast Guard was here! That was an answer to prayers she hadn't even thought of. She'd assumed the traffickers would take them south, not toward American waters.

"We need to be ready," she instructed Daniel.

"What can we do?"

She woke up the children. "Someone is coming to rescue us. Be quiet and be ready to move."

They both nodded, their eyes wide with fear. It'd been a miracle they'd fallen asleep earlier. She stood and took the baby from Daniel. Their room was locked from the outside. She didn't know how she could escape, but she was going to be ready to help if she could.

Shots rang out from above, and she gasped. She handed the baby back to Daniel and ushered them behind her along the wall. Searching around the room, her eyes landed on the lamp. It was all they had. She ripped it from the wall and threw the lampshade away. They were in complete darkness now, but that would hopefully be to their advantage.

Waiting by the door, she prayed when it opened she'd know if she should smack the person or hug them.

The shots stopped, and footsteps pounded down the hallway. She heard the key turn in the lock and waited, heart in her throat.

The door swung slowly inward, and the hallway light silhouetted a man with a gun held in front of him. Sydnee didn't think the Coast Guard would approach like this. She swung the lamp down on those arms with every bit of strength she had.

The man cursed in Spanish and the gun flew across the room. Sydnee's eyes widened when she realized it was the trafficker who had attacked her and Daniel originally and tonight had come back for them. He turned and grabbed for her. She tried to dodge, but he wrapped his hands around her neck and in one quick movement, slammed her face first onto the carpeted floor. Sydnee cried out, pain ripping through her face, elbows, and knees. Her head was cloudy and her stomach rolled. The man jumped on top of her, pummeling her with his hard fists in the back of the neck and head.

"He came for you," he yelled, "but I'll kill you before he finds you!"

Sydnee gasped. The world spun one way, then another as successive punches landed from both directions. She was disoriented and dealing with too much pain to clear her head. Who had come for her? Brooks? The hope gave her strength she didn't know she had. She bucked her body like a wild steer and threw the man to the side. Rolling onto her stomach, she vomited.

Every part of her wanted to lose consciousness and sink to the floor, but her children were defenseless. Slowly pushing to her knees as if she were underwater and trying to surface, she saw Daniel gouging his fingers into the man's eyes and Alejandro pulling the dude's hair.

A large shadow appeared at the door. Sydnee glanced up, and all the air whooshed out of her. "Brooks," she whispered. He looked fiercely handsome in his black clothes, with weapons strapped over his chest and around his waist. The fury on his face was palatable.

He grabbed the guy and yanked him to his feet, then slammed him against the wall, leaving an imprint of his body in the old paneling. Daniel and Alejandro backed up. María held Tomás, who howled his protests. Sydnee struggled to her feet, bracing herself against the bed frame.

Brooks held on to the man with one hand and punched him in the face. The man whined and raised his hands, trying to deflect the barrage. But Brooks was like a machine, a black belt in action. With hands, elbows, and knees he pounded on the man as if he was nothing more than a practice dummy, then easily tossed him headfirst into the other wall of the room.

Brooks' eyes immediately focused on Sydnee. She self-consciously pushed the hair back from her face, wiped her lips clean, and winced at the pounding in her head. She must look horrible, but who cared? Brooks had come for them.

"Are you okay?" he asked, his voice unsteady.

"No, but you're here now." Sydnee stumbled into his arms. He caught her easily and pulled her into a hard embrace before giving her a kiss that would've won a blue ribbon at the county fair. Passion, safety, and love wrapped around her. She probably tasted horrible, but he didn't seem to mind.

"Meester!" Daniel screamed.

The trafficker launched himself onto Brooks's back and wrapped his arms around his neck. It was the same hold Sydnee had used to choke out the other trafficker, so she knew a smaller, weaker person could do some serious damage with it.

Sydnee grabbed at the man's hands and tried to unlatch them. Brooks spun away from Sydnee and dropped backward to the floor, smashing the man beneath him. He ripped the man's hands away and flipped over. Jumping up, he pulled the man to his feet and gave him a hard uppercut to the jaw.

"You want to go again?" Brooks asked.

"No!" The man shielded his face with his hands.

José appeared in the doorframe. "Can I take that garbage from you, boss?"

"Thank you, my friend." Brooks shoved the trafficker out the door. José wrenched the man's hands behind his back and dragged him up the hallway.

Brooks exhaled and turned back to Sydnee. "Where were we?"

Sydnee laughed, relief coursing through her body and the pain in her head lessening. "Well, you'd just saved me and I was giving you a kiss of gratitude."

"Let's try the kiss again." Brooks winked, hugged her to him, and gave her a quick peck on the lips.

"Oh, Brooks, I'm so sorry."

"You're sorry?"

"I was so wrong to demand you be with the children, when you obviously needed me to understand what you've been through and not push you into something you're not comfortable with." It was too much to explain and apologize for, so she simply said, "I choose you, Brooks, always you."

He smiled down at her. "I choose you too, love."

She kissed him again.

The crying baby drew Sydnee back. She reluctantly pulled away from Brook's arms. "I'll take him," she told Mariá.

Brooks reached for Tomás before Sydnee could. The little one calmed almost immediately, staring up at the huge man as if he wasn't sure if he should be scared or comforted. Sydnee blinked, not certain if she was seeing this correctly. Her heart beat faster, and she kept telling herself not to get her hopes up.

Brooks smiled down at the baby and bounced slightly. "It's okay, little one. I've got you."

Daniel and Alejandro watched Brooks with worshipful gazes. Mariá looked terrified of the entire situation. Sydnee pulled her against her side. "We're safe now, sweetie. This is Mr. Hoffman, the man who provides the money for the orphanage." She glanced up and noted that Brooks watched her, seeming to consider her every word. "He's the best man I know, and he'll make sure no one hurts us."

Brooks swallowed and smiled at Mariá. "That's right, love. You're safe now."

Baby Tomás took to Brooks immediately, exploring Brooks's strong jaw with his chubby fingers and cooing at him.

"Meester Hoffman, sir," Daniel said.

"Yes?"

"You are a bad a—"

"Daniel!" Sydnee cried out.

"I mean a tough guy."

Brooks threw his head back and laughed. "Thank you, son." His eyes widened as if he'd just realized what he'd said. "You were doing a good job of taking care of everyone without me, though."

Daniel puffed out his thin chest. Alejandro patted his friend's shoulder. "You'll never be as tough as Meester Hoffman."

They all laughed. It felt so good after the fear of the past few hours.

"Would you train me, Meester Hoffman? To be tough like you and to fight like you?" With all seriousness, Daniel raised his fists as if ready to fight.

Brooks looked over the young boy, then made eye contact with Sydnee. She waited with bated breath. Was this the step Brooks needed, or would it send him into a panic? He seemed calm and ready to try. "Yes, son. I will."

"Sweet!" Daniel and Alejandro bumped fists.

Sydnee released a sigh. She leaned closer to Brooks. "You've never been more attractive to me."

"Really?" He quirked an eyebrow. "Hold a baby and you want me, eh?"

"You have no idea."

Brooks pulled her into his side, bent down, and kissed her lips. "Merry Christmas, love."

"I forgot all about Christmas! I don't even have a present for you."

"I'm sure it's impossible to find the perfect present for the perfect man. I just want an hour alone with those lips." Brooks winked at her.

"That sounds good, but ..." She licked her lips and admitted, "I do like presents."

He chuckled. "Then we're both in luck. I have a pile of presents hidden away just for my girl."

Sydnee smiled. She liked the sound of that.

"One question, though." His brow furrowed. "We aren't going to see that Jace guy again?"

Sydnee batted her eyelashes. "Someone's jealous."

"Do I need to be?"

"No, love." She kissed him. "We won't see him again until we go visit my family in Alabama."

"Introducing me to the family?" Brooks' eyebrows lifted. "Hmm, somebody's serious about this relationship."

"You have no idea."

"I might have a little."

He bounced the baby slightly and ushered the rest of them out of the door, up the stairs, and to the safety of his yacht. Relief and love swept through Sydnee. She glanced over at their handsome rescuer giving instructions to his men, securing the traffickers, and holding a baby. He'd forgiven her so quickly for being such a pigheaded brat. She'd spend as long as it took showing him that he was worthy of love and so much more. By his side was where she belonged.

CHAPTER TWENTY-THREE

They were able to rescue ten other children. José took them to the authorities while Sydnee and her four little ones—and Brooks—returned to the orphanage in time for Christmas morning. Brooks and Sydnee sat cuddled on a couch, watching the children unwrap the huge pile of presents he'd bought for them, and then the children dove into the much smaller pile Sydnee, Camila, and Rosmerta had been assembling for months.

The children all took turns thanking Brooks. Sydnee noticed he was a little reluctant, like a puppy who splashed in a puddle for the first time. He liked it, but wasn't ready to go dive in the big pool. She made sure to stay close and direct the focus off of him when he seemed uncomfortable.

Tomás hadn't left his arms, and after the baby had downed a bottle, he'd fallen asleep. Brooks held on to him, and Sydnee caught him several times gazing down at the baby with a look of wonder. She really did think Brooks looked amazing with the innocent baby cuddled in his strong arms, but she hoped they weren't pushing too fast. The trauma from his youth wasn't going to be healed quickly, but she was beyond grateful that he was willing to try.

The gathering room was a mess of wrapping paper and toys, but nobody seemed to care. The children played happily until Camila insisted they all needed to eat the Christmas breakfast Brooks's cook, Valentina, had prepared. Brooks and Sydnee stood. Tomás' head lolled to the side.

"He looks as tired as I feel," Sydnee said. "Let me go lay him down."

"Okay."

Brooks handed over the baby. Did she dare hope he was a bit reluctant to do so? Sydnee carried Tomás to the nursery and laid him down with a kiss on his soft cheek. He needed a bath almost as much as she did, but they could worry about that when he woke up.

She turned, and Brooks was leaning against the doorframe, watching her. Smiling, she walked straight to him, stood on tiptoes, and kissed him. "I love you, Brooks."

He pulled her against his chest. "I love you, Sydnee. Let's agree from now on that I'm always right so we never have to fight."

Sydnee laughed. "That sounds like a plan ... in your dreams."

Brooks groaned. "Okay, you can be right, but you have to always kiss me better."

"I can do that."

He wrapped his arm around her and walked with her down the hallway. "Camila told me to get you out of here for a little bit."

"She did?"

"I might have mentioned you haven't opened your presents from me."

Sydnee bit at her lower lip. She could hardly wait. It took almost twenty minutes and many promises that they would return quickly to say goodbye to the children. Daniel and Alejandro's droopy faces made Sydnee feel like they were deserting them. She caught a glance at Brooks and could sense he didn't like seeing them uncertain or unhappy. His palm against hers was sweaty.

"I promise I'll be back by lunchtime. You have fun with your toys," she tried.

Daniel kicked at the floor. "I'm too old for toys."

Brooks' brow wrinkled. She wondered if he'd ever been given toys. Hopefully from Mr. Hoffman, but she didn't know that. How could she comfort Daniel while still showing Brooks that he would come first for her?

Brooks took a deep breath and stepped forward, releasing her hand and bending down to Daniel's level. "Remember how I promised to teach you how to fight?"

Daniel nodded.

"I'm going to give you your own knife too, but you'll have to use it at my house."

Daniel's eyes widened. He flung himself against Brooks. "Thank you!"

Brooks jumped, but awkwardly patted the boy on the shoulder. Daniel and Alejandro said their goodbyes and went to fill their plates with sausage.

Brooks escorted Sydnee to his Hummer, then drove quickly to his house. He tapped his fingers on the steering wheel, and his leg bounced.

"You okay?" Sydnee asked. "You seem ... nervous." She didn't know if she'd ever seen Brooks nervous.

"Daniel is happy, isn't he?"

"I believe so. He takes the responsibility of being the oldest very seriously, but he's doing good at school and he smiles a lot. You should see him play soccer. He's really lit up then."

"You're a little angel with a bite, you know?"

"Not sure that was a compliment."

"It was. You help and love everyone, but you aren't a pushover."

He reached over and took her hand, kissing her knuckles, then resting their clasped hands on his muscled thigh. Sydnee reclined her head against the headrest. She was exhausted, but being with Brooks kept her awake and then some.

They pulled into his house, and several of his staff were waiting with questions, hugs, and reassurances that they'd been praying all night. Brooks treated them like his best friends, taking the time to make each one feel important. Sydnee wondered why she'd ever doubted this man. His goodness and sincerity shone through. He took her up to his bedroom, and she was a bit in awe at the massive suite.

"I've never brought a woman in here before."

Sydnee blinked at him. "Never?"

"No, love."

"Maddie told me to ask about your conversion story."

Brooks took her hand and led her to a couch that overlooked the ocean. They sat, and he said, "Mr. Hoffman always read to me from the Bible and expected me to go to church and say my prayers, but you know me, of course I rebelled. I'd rather fight someone than pray over them.

"My senior year of college, I found some men ..." He cleared his throat and glanced at her, then away. "Taking advantage of a woman. I fought them and ..." He exhaled slowly.

"You don't have to tell me if it's too hard," Sydnee reassured him, still feeling guilty for her lack of understanding about the childhood issues that made him so uncertain around her children. She didn't want to unearth more painful memories.

"It's hard, but I can tell you." He clenched and unclenched his fist. "I was out of control; I was so upset for what they'd done to the woman." He shuddered, and Sydnee didn't even want to know what they'd done to the woman. Brooks focused on the floor and said, "I injured one of them so badly ... he's a paraplegic now."

Sydnee placed a hand over her mouth, but not quick enough to hold in the gasp. She wrapped her arms around his broad shoulders and held on.

He glanced at her. "I was never prosecuted. Four against one and they put the woman in the hospital and ruined any chance of her ever having children." He was clenching his fist again.

Sydnee gently massaged his shoulders, uncertain if she should talk or let him get this out.

"I couldn't forgive myself. Mr. Hoffman taught me how to turn even something as horrible as that over to the Savior. It took me months of study and prayer, but I finally did get to know Him and was able to find mercy. I visited the man in the hospital, and he granted his forgiveness." He shook his head. "We're both changed people and keep in touch. Mr. Hoffman helped him get through school, and he's a corrections officer in Fresno now. And I committed myself to be pure, kind, and always watch out for those in need."

Sydnee pulled him close. They sat in contemplative silence for a few minutes. "Thank you for sharing. You're pretty amazing, you know that?"

"Ah." Brooks gave her his overconfident grin. "Took you long enough to figure that out."

Sydnee laughed. "Guess I'm a slow learner."

"As long as you got there."

She wrapped her arms around his neck and gave him a lingering kiss. "You were so quick to forgive me for being a bully and misunderstanding you. I'm sorry it was so hard to forgive yourself."

"You're a lot more fun to forgive." He stood. "I think it's time for presents."

She rubbed her hands together, and he chuckled. Brooks strode to the closet and came back with a pile of wrapped gifts. He set them on the table in front of her. "I didn't know if you'd even want these from me."

"A girl always wants presents, no matter who they're from."

"I feel reassured."

"I wish I had something for you."

"I told you, lots of hugs and kisses."

She grinned and reached for a small box on the top of the pile.

"That one's last." Brooks took it from her and held on to it as she ripped into the beautifully wrapped gifts.

Dresses, scarves, perfume, necklaces, chocolates, and purses all got unwrapped. Sydnee hugged him after she opened each present. "Thank you! I love it!"

Brooks' grin was wide. "I love this reaction. I'll buy you gifts every day."

"Don't. You'll spoil me." She started piling presents on the coffee table and wadding up wrapping paper.

"You forgot one," Brooks said.

Her eyes flew to the box in his hand. She was suddenly nervous. It was the right shape, but it couldn't be, could it? "You've already given me so much."

"I've given you my heart." Brooks winked.

"Oh, that was cheesy."

He chuckled and placed the small box in her hands. Sydnee carefully pulled the bow off, then unwrapped the box. It was a velvet jewelry box. She glanced up at him. "Brooks," she whispered.

He took a quick breath, his smile a little lopsided. "This is my moment to woo you, my love." He took the box from her hand and knelt down next to the couch. "I love you, Sydnee. I can't imagine how you'd find any happiness without me."

She laughed at his wording, but her heart was hammering out of control.

He popped the lid, and the brilliance of a huge teardrop diamond almost blinded her. "Will you marry me?"

Sydnee wrapped her arm around his neck and pulled him to her. "Yes!" She kissed him, then wiped the tears from her eyes. Brooks gently put the ring on her finger. She studied the diamond-studded gold band that encased the large center diamond.

They held each other for a few minutes, not saying anything. Brooks pulled back first. "I've looked for you my entire life, love."

Sydnee grinned. "I can't imagine loving anyone more than you."

Brooks laughed. "I don't know about that. I've seen the way you look at that fat baby."

The mention of Tomás brought a pang to her heart. If she married Brooks, she would have to leave the orphanage and all those children that she loved so much. "Brooks?" she whispered.

He sighed heavily and wrapped his hands around hers. "I've been thinking much too hard about a solution, my love. Let's get married and then see about adopting Daniel, Alejandro, and Tomás."

"Brooks?" Was she in a dream? She stared at him in shock. Did he realize what he was saying? Was he really ready for this?

"You look so cute when you're perplexed, my love."

"Oh, Brooks. Are you sure? I don't want you to do this just for me." She pressed a fist against her mouth, fighting back tears.

"I'd do anything for you, and I know I couldn't ask you to leave them. We'll still fund the orphanage and go visit the rest of the children whenever you want, but I know those three are really special to you. I want to train Daniel not just to fight, but to take over my businesses."

"Are you going to be Mr. Hoffman to him?"

"No, I could never do that." The fear splashed across Brooks' face again.

Oh no. He was only talking about adoption for her. She was allowing her desire for her children to overshadow what was best for Brooks. Again. "You don't need to adopt them, Brooks. I can volunteer at the orphanage every day and come home to you each night. We'll make it work."

"Yeah, we will make it work because I'm not going to be Mr. Hoffman to them." He nodded and gave her his easy grin. "I'm going to be Papa."

She threw herself against his chest. "Are you sure?"

"Yes. I love Zack and Maddie's children; I'm sure I can love my own."

The tears leaked out then, and she stifled a sob. "I love you. I love you so much."

"There's a lot of me to love."

Sydnee laughed and shook her head. "Your heart is every bit as big as your head."

"And neither of those are as big as my biceps." He gave her a squeeze that made her lightheaded, then bowed his head to hers. "But my lips are the best part about me."

"Finally, something we can agree on." She giggled. Brooks stifled it with those perfect lips.

ABOUT THE AUTHOR

Cami is a part-time author, part-time exercise consultant, part-time housekeeper, full-time wife, and overtime mother of four adorable boys. Sleep and relaxation are fond memories. She's never been happier.

Sign up for Cami's newsletter to receive a free ebook copy of *The Feisty One: A Billionaire Bride Pact Romance* and information about new releases, discounts, and promotions here.

If you enjoyed *Cozumel Escape,* please read on for a sneak peek at Sydnee's friend, Jace's story in *Cancun Getaway.*

www.camichecketts.com
cami@camichecketts.com

EXCERPT FROM CANCUN GETAWAY

Moriah tilted her head back and let the sun kiss her face. They'd landed in Cancun two hours ago, and a driver had brought them and their friends Trin and Zander straight to the upscale, all-inclusive resort. She and her three-year old, Turk, had changed into their suits first thing and headed straight for the beach. They were having the time of their lives digging in the sand.

The resort was massive. The buildings housing the rooms had eight or nine floors, depending on if they boasted a penthouse or not. The resort was shaped like a horseshoe with the open end to the beach. All of the pools, restaurants, and spa area were in the center. The beach was just a flight of stairs below the pools, separated by a retaining wall, waterfalls, and infinity pools, with most of the pools and rooms over-looking the glorious ocean. Yay for paradise.

"Shovel, Mama!" Turk commanded.

"Demanding, demanding." Moriah knelt on the sand and put a hand on her hip, tossing her black curls. "You don't boss *the* Mama around."

Turk giggled. "*Please* shovel, Mama. I need tracks for my monster truck."

She smiled and dug in. His track was already extensive, but she'd do anything for her little man. As Turk pushed the truck around the track making zoom noises, Moriah savored the sound of the waves. Living in Montgomery, Alabama her entire life, she'd made it to Gulf Shores a few times. It wasn't like this was her first time at the ocean, but it was definitely her first time on white-sand-Caribbean beaches, and she was in heaven.

Trin and Zander hadn't made it down from their room yet. *Dang newly-married lovers,* she thought, but she was happy for them. She couldn't believe they'd talked her into leaving the bed and breakfast for over a week. Trin and Zander owned the Cloverdale. The mansion had been in Trin's family for generations, and Moriah felt like the restored bed and breakfast was her home too, and Trin was closer to her than family. In fact, they liked to claim they were sisters just to see people's reactions. Moriah smiled thinking about people's reactions. Trin was a tall, beautiful redhead, and Moriah was petite and as brown as her mama's mahogany bookcases.

A group of young adults were playing volleyball about fifty yards down the beach, and Moriah found her gaze drawn in that direction. Three of the men looked like they could be triplets from this distance—tall, blond, and too good-looking for their own good. Her brother Harrison was always teasing her that she had vanilla fever, but he knew better than anybody that blond men just spelled heartache and trouble for her. Why was it they could steal her eyeballs from their intended target? A pair of nice blue eyes could give her heart palpitations. It didn't help that she never had time to date and hardly met any single men her age working in a bed and breakfast that catered to couples. Luckily, she always stayed strong where blond men were concerned, or at least, she had for the past three years.

One of the men glanced her way for a third time and gave her a broad smile. His teal-blue eyes were beckoning to her as his tanned cheek crinkled with an irresistible grin. Moriah returned the smile, but quickly refocused on digging the track. Sheesh, she thought she was used to heat and humidity, but she was suddenly burning up. *Lord, give me strength to resist the white hottie.* She chuckled to herself. As if the man was going to chase her around the resort. There were plenty of women taking part in the volleyball game who looked more than happy to hang on his every muscle.

"Mama, look." Turk pointed out at the gently rolling waves where some teenage girls were trying to stand up on paddleboards. They squealed as a larger wave came along and knocked both of them into the water.

"Let's do that," Turk said.

Moriah sprang up. She was more than ready to try anything and everything in this tropical paradise. Volleyball topped the list, even though she wasn't any good at the actual sport. She chanced another glance at her blond Adonis. Just her luck that he was serving the ball at that moment. His muscles rippled underneath his tanned skin. A moment later, the other team returned his serve. He dove to save the ball, and she had to look away or risk diving after him herself.

He stood, brushing sand from his shredded abdomen and then caught her eye again. Oh. My. Goodness. Hopefully, paddle boarding would cool her off. A tall redhead bee-bopped up to Moriah's Adonis and placed her hands on his chest, drawing his attention away from Moriah. Of course he had women draping themselves all over him. Look at the guy.

Turk was already skipping down the beach in the opposite direction of the volleyball net. Moriah hurried after him and found the resort worker who provided beach equipment. Within minutes, they had lifejackets, instructions, a paddle, and a long board in the water that was, unfortunately, not one bit stable.

Moriah placed Turk on the board then knelt behind him, grasping the paddle. They were only inches deep, and one wave shot them back onto the beach.

"Come on, Mama. Let's go." Turk demanded.

"I'm trying, little man." Moriah pushed off the sand hard with the paddle, and they moved a few feet. She started paddling ferociously but had to lift the paddle to the other side of the board and over Turk's head every few strokes. They'd turn one direction then the other and were making very little progress as waves kept pushing them in. She needed to stand up to paddle more effectively and make any headway against the gentle waves.

"Okay, buddy. Hold on." They were only in a foot of water so it wouldn't matter if they tipped, but it felt awkward, as if the people in lounge chairs on the beach were watching them. What about her volleyball-playing Adonis? She hoped he wasn't anywhere nearby.

Slowly, she stood, flexing her abs to help her balance. Her legs trembled, and she couldn't even think about paddling. She simply tried to stay upright. A wave rolled toward them. As it lifted one side of the board, Moriah let out a yelp, but she rode through it and miraculously didn't fall in. Turk was cheering. "Yeah!"

"Whew. That was a close one."

"Good job, Mama. Now, can you *please* paddle faster? I wanna surf!"

"I'll try." She doubted they'd do anything close to surfing, but she had to try for her boy. Shakily, she inserted the paddle into the water and pushed off the sand. Her legs wobbled. They moved a few inches. Moriah lifted the paddle to the other side. The board bobbed and, before she could do much more than cry out, flipped them both off.

Moriah was able to stay on her feet and only landed in a foot of water. Turk got dunked, but his life jacket kept him floating. She hurriedly grabbed him and lifted him out. "Are you okay?"

Turk grinned. "We're bad at this, Mama."

She laughed. "Yes, my man, we are."

"Would you like a little help?" a deep voice asked from behind her. Moriah whirled around, and her eyes widened. Adonis had been good from afar, but he was miles past good up close. She brushed the curls from her face and swallowed hard.

"We're just newbies, but we're scrappy. We'll figure it out." She arched an eyebrow and gave him a saucy swirl of her hips. It wasn't a conscious flirtation, just natural instinct. Trin always teased her that she danced her way through life.

He grinned, set his paddle on his board, and pushed it back onto the beach. How had he gotten a board without her even noticing? He had a lifejacket on so at least his chest and abdomen was covered, but his shoulders and arms were picture-perfect enough to make her need one of those specialty drinks the waiters kept offering. "Wouldn't it be more fun to try it together?"

"If you're sure you're up for a lesson." Did he have a slight Southern accent? His voice reminded her of somebody who'd grown up in the South then had it knocked out of them by Northern schooling and a rich lifestyle.

"No issue sharing my expertise with a beautiful woman."

"I meant me teaching you." She pointed her finger at him, grinning at her sauciness. Of course, she couldn't teach him anything but dance moves.

"Oh?" He chuckled easily. "I like the sound of that." Wading into the water, he held out his arms to her boy. "Do you want to ride with me, buddy? Then your sister will have an easier time teaching us how it's done."

Moriah opened her mouth to correct his assumption. She wasn't surprised as she was mistaken for Turk's sister and aunt a lot. Unfortunately, Turk interrupted her. "Sure!" He hollered.

Moriah loved how Turk's "sure" always came out as a happy "shore." As he launched himself into the man's arms, Moriah scrambled for her boy, but came up empty. Turk was naturally friendly with everyone, but he especially loved large men who tossed him in the air.

Moriah stared at the two of them together, and the world around her seemed to settle. The tall, good-looking, tanned man holding her little boy with his smooth, brown skin and curly hair made quite the picture. She wished she was a painter and could capture this moment. The contrast of the man and her child, yet the absolute rightness of them both, combined with the beach and the ocean was simply beautiful.

Adonis pulled his board out and settled Turk on it, handing him the large paddle. "How old are you, buddy?"

"Me three!" Turk called out happily.

"I think that's big enough to steer for a minute while I help the beautiful lady. Then I'll come take you into the deep water."

"Okay. Sure."

The way Turk said "shore" was so stinking cute it brought a quick smile to Adonis' face. Moriah had to clench her hands to keep from reaching out and touching that bronzed cheek. Adonis turned to her, and her breath caught in her throat.

"Okay. Let me help you up."

"I told you I've got it," Moriah said quickly, scrambling onto the board with the paddle in hand. It tipped one way and then the other, and before she could react, she was in the water again. Adonis caught her around the waist. Moriah looked up, and those blue eyes twinkled at her. "Oh, Lord have mercy." She muttered.

His grin widened as he plucked her up out of the water like she was a sack of sugar and planted her on the board. It wobbled, but he kept her steady. Moriah glanced over at Turk who was happily splashing with his paddle just a few feet away. Adonis' hands were at her waist as he reached up to help her. He kept his gaze on her face as he moved his hands to just above her knees. Moriah gasped. If there was a more sensual move or way a man could look at a woman, she sure hadn't seen or experienced it.

It was definitely time for some sass. She was in danger of falling for the tall hottie before she even learned his name and possibly throwing herself into a bigger mess than the last one she'd been in with a blue-eyed blond. She was older now and much more mature and sensible, so she couldn't fall into that trap again, right?

"I think you can take your hands off, thank you very much," she said as tartly as she could.

His eyebrows lifted. "You sure you ready to fly solo?"

"Been doing it my whole life."

"Really? Why?"

He still hadn't removed his stinking hands from her legs, and she was quivering with the wonderful sensation of it all. Thankfully, Turk was oblivious, happily patting the water and singing to himself.

"When you reach mama status at seventeen, you grow up fast." She pinned him with a look. There, that should stop his flirting. She was a mama, and no matter how challenging the path to sunshine had been, she was proud of Turk and thrilled with every moment of her life now. She was also very leery where good-looking blond men were concerned.

"You're a mother?" Finally, his hands dropped. Fortunately, she didn't plummet into the water, but stayed swaying on the board.

He looked over at Turk then back at her. His jaw low. "No, really? I thought maybe a nephew or brother."

She fell off the stinking board again, splashing into the water next to him. "Nope, he's my boy. Come on, Turk. Let's go."

"No, Mama, we didn't have a ride."

"We can't crush a little boy's dreams." Adonis winked at her then waded through the water to where Turk perched on his board. The man pushed away from the shore, easily stepped up behind Turk, and started paddling away.

"W-wait." Moriah had frozen when he left her in the shallow water. She quickly regained her senses, knelt on her board, and paddled to try to keep up. Again, she went one direction then another, but she couldn't get anywhere close to him.

Turk laughed gleefully as they zoomed over waves and out past the buoys.

"Slow down!" She screamed at the man's broad, retreating shoulders. She knew he wasn't really going to steal her child, but it just felt wrong that she wasn't right next to Turk.

Adonis glanced over his shoulder and smirked at her. "You're looking great."

The nerve, the absolute nerve of the man.

"Come on, Mama." Turk called happily. "Whee! I'm surfing." He put his chubby arms out and laughed so cutely.

"You're not supposed to go past the buoys." She hollered at Adonis' back.

The man turned a smooth circle and stroked easily back toward her. His board bumped into hers, and Turk laughed. Moriah stayed on her knees, relief whooshing through her. She didn't like her son to be too far away.

"Sorry. I didn't hear that rule," he said, looking unrepentant as he grinned at her.

Moriah was mad, which was completely unlike her. She always rolled with life and kept a smile on her face, but right now, this guy ticked her off. Taking off with her boy like that was completely out of line. "Don't you dare try to steal my boy or I'll hogtie you and beat you with a stick."

"Where are you from?" he asked. Rather than scare him, her threats seemed to create more interest in his eyes.

"Excuse me?" What did that have to do with the price of bacon?

"You talk like home."

Before he'd taken off with her child, back when he had those strong hands on her waist and then her legs, she'd felt a sense of home from him too.

"Montgomery, Alabama." She lifted her chin. Proud as proud could be of her Southern upbringing.

"I'm from Mountain Green."

"Figures." She spat. "All the rich hotties live there." Mountain Green was an ultra-wealthy suburb of Birmingham, about an hour and a half north of her home.

He lifted an eyebrow.

"Let's surf, Mister." Turk pounded on the surfboard with his open palms.

"Do you care if we go on another ride if we stay within the buoys?"

"Thank you for having the courtesy to ask this time."

He grinned. "Sometimes us rich hotties remember our social graces."

A laugh erupted from her before she could contain it. The man stared at her. It was one of those intense, sensual looks she'd only seen in the movies and sometimes when she caught Zander staring at her friend, Trin. It dried up her laughter quickly, and she wondered if she needed to jump off her board and into the ocean.

"Do that again." He murmured.

"What?" She pushed at her curly locks.

"Laugh."

"Why?"

"That was the most beautiful sound I've ever heard."

A charmer too, Moriah thought as warmth darted through her. Just like that, he'd taken away her frustrations, but at the same time terrified her. Turk's daddy, Brock, had also been a charmer.

Read more or buy *Cancun Getaway* here.

EXCERPT FROM CARIBBEAN RESCUE

by Cami Checketts

Madeline Panetto rushed down the lower hallway of the yacht, praying she wouldn't run into one of her father's men. A hand snaked around her arm and pulled her to a stop. Madeline swung a fist and connected with a muscular shoulder. The man grunted and yanked her against his chest.

"Don't worry, la mia bella donna." Bello breathed into her neck. Maddie cringed, wanting to punch him again. "It is only me."

He was exactly who she'd been hoping to avoid. Bello made her skin crawl with his insinuations that she should be into him. Where was her father when she needed him? Bello had been quick to tell Maddie that his name meant handsome in Italian as he gave her a leering wink. During the past week and a half, she'd worked hard to avoid his wandering hands and suggestive looks, but it was a full-time job. He was handsome, tall, and dark, but his soul was twisted and ugly. She'd figured out his true character within her first five minutes on the yacht and changed his name to Bello the Barbaric. It had a nice rhythm, and it completely fit.

"I need to get dressed for dinner." Maddie succeeded in pulling her arm free.

"I could help you change." Bello winked and trailed his fingers along her collarbone.

Maddie shivered and backed up a step. "I'm a big girl; I think I can handle it."

"You are a big girl." His eyes slithered over her body.

Yuck. Maddie felt like she'd been dunked in a tub of manure.

"You know, every time we ... stop a boat ..." He cleared his throat and grinned like they were sharing some secret, like she didn't know what kind of vicious and despicable scumball he was. "The women beg for me to take care of them. I think you'll find you enjoy the experience."

Maddie barely stopped herself from slapping him. Hands trembling with rage at what those poor women had gone through—what she might go through if she didn't get off this ship—she scurried around him and ran down the hallway. Tripping on nothing, she righted herself quickly and kept moving.

"See you at dinner. I hope you're wearing something special for me."

"I hope you burn in purgatory!" Maddie screamed back, hating the smirk on his lips and knowing look in his eyes. He was going to force himself on her if she wasn't very, very careful.

Her heart rate didn't return to normal until she reached her own room and locked the door. Dressing quickly, she secured the heavy diamond necklace around her throat; a graduation gift from her father. She wished she could avoid facing Bello at dinner, but she'd be safe if she stayed close to her father. Bello acted like a gentleman when his boss was within ear's length.

She checked her reflection, liking the floor-length, teal-colored lace dress. Teal worked with her dark hair and olive skin. She supposed she was a good combination of her Italian father and Spanish mother, but hoped she was nothing like them in moral structure. Maybe it was wrong to blame her mother for lying to her for twenty-four years. She had been a decent single parent and a good example of a hardworking, well-educated woman, but the lying ... It made Maddie want to disown both her parents.

The luxurious Sussurro Yacht swayed slightly, but she'd gotten used to that after a few days. If only she could get used to being around her father and the awful men he called friends, business associates, pirate mates, mafia connections. Which name fit?

Maddie shuddered. Her father was a pirate. *Didn't see that one coming.* She'd never thought of herself as thick-headed, but obviously she must have been not to have realized who or what her father was and then agree to sail around the Caribbean with him as a graduation present. Oh, to go back to the simplicity of college life. Her master's thesis had been much easier than this ploy of a trip. Faking that she was comfortable around Bello the Butthole made her want to wear baggy sweats to dinner and pretend she was deaf. But that wasn't possible. Instead, she'd have to dress appropriately in her diamond necklace and Bergdorf Goodman evening gown—which was ridiculous, considering the price tag was probably over seven grand.

Loud bangs and thumps came from above. Maddie jerked and glanced at the ceiling as if it had the answer to the sudden disturbance. A gunshot rang out. Maddie ducked instinctively. Terror pricked at her spine as her hands grew clammy and her body trembled.

Where could she go to be safe? They'd look in the closet, and the bed frame was attached to the floor. Could she jump overboard and hope she could make it to one of the many Caribbean islands? Oh, man! She'd been ticked at her father off and on throughout her life, usually because she wanted his attention and he wasn't around, but at this moment, she truly hated him. Maybe she'd get lucky and her father's employees would shoot each other and leave her alone. Maybe this was just another idiotic way these men passed the time. The only reason they hadn't used her to pass the time was that her father would've slit their throats. *Piece of dung pirates.*

Maddie grabbed a heavy picture frame off the table and crept toward the door. She wasn't going to sit here and wait for somebody to come kill her. The walkie-talkie her father had given her to communicate onboard the ship buzzed as more shots and some loud thumps came from above. "Madeline," her father panted out. "Meet me at my room. Now."

"Is everything—" she started, but he'd clicked off.

Maddie clung to the walkie-talkie and the picture frame and slowly opened her door. There was no sound in the hallway. Hopefully all the action was upstairs, and she could make it down the passageway to her father's room without being shot.

Another gun discharged, and she jumped and screamed. *Forget caution.* She sprinted down the hall—not an easy feat in a tight evening gown. A rip of fabric informed her she'd damaged the dress. The only reason she cared was that she'd hoped to resell the gowns to fund some humanitarian trips.

She banged through the door and into the suite at the rear of the boat. This yacht was massive. She'd never seen anything like it except on those television specials where they toured ridiculously wealthy people's homes and yachts.

Thankfully, her father's room was quiet and dark. She didn't dare flip on the lights, but called out softly, "Papa?" It wasn't a term of endearment anymore, just what he'd expected her to call him during his infrequent visits. She'd taken to calling him *father* the past few years to tick him off, but in her terror, the old term came out.

No answer.

Maddie shut the door behind her and turned on a side lamp, not wanting the bright overhead light on. She set her picture frame down and crept toward his safe. He'd told her the combination when he gave her a tour of the ship and told her to take out the weapons, money, papers sealed in a waterproof packet, and the flash drive if there was ever an emergency.

She wondered if they'd been attacked by another pirate ship; apparently there were a whole slew of them. Maybe his troops had started an uprising. Her father controlled them with an iron fist, and the fear in his staff's eyes made her sick. Maybe they were finished being afraid.

Quickly unlocking the safe, she pulled out a pistol first and inserted bullets into the chamber. Her hands only shook slightly. One of the few things her father had taught her when he'd visited—besides the fact he adored her mother, and Maddie was an unfortunate by-product of their romance—was how to shoot a sidearm.

The door cracked open. Maddie whirled, her finger tightening on the trigger.

"It's me," her father, Armando, whispered, sliding into the room. "Nice job getting the revolver." He slid the deadbolt to secure the door, then pushed a heavy dresser in front of it.

Maddie's arm slackened to her side as she watched him. Finally, she found her voice. "What's going on?"

"Bello has made his play."

"I thought you trusted him. You said he was like a son to you." Her voice escalated with her terror.

"Lesson learned. Never trust anyone, my love."

He had no right to use terms of endearment. "What does he want?"

"My money. My power." He shook his head and strode past her to the safe, muttering, "And you."

Maddie's entire body shuddered. She'd rather be ripped apart by a shark; at least she could retain her virtue and self-respect. "And you're just going to barricade us in here and hope he changes his mind? Great plan, Pops."

"I've got a better one." He pulled the flash drive that was sealed in plastic out of the safe and handed it to her. "This is the most important thing I will ever give you. Keep it safe until you can turn it over to Homeland Security. Hide it where you won't lose it."

Maddie tucked it into her bra.

"Good girl." He entered a code and then yanked open a side door. Maddie found herself looking at a small boat. "Get in. Bello and I had planned to have you take the papers and flash drive to America when we dropped you off in San Juan next week and make us honest men, but apparently he has other plans. At least he doesn't know about the escape boat. It's nothing fancy, but should get you to the nearest island. Go west or south." He actually smiled like this was funny.

Maddie's stomach dropped. How was she supposed to know what direction to go in the dark? "Me or us?"

"Only you. I'll hold them off as long as I can." Her father shoved the sealed bag into her hands. "This is a paper copy of everything on the drive, some cash, and several different passports, social security cards, and birth certificates for you and your mother."

"What? Reverse a minute. Go back to why you aren't coming with me." She didn't like her father, but she didn't want Bello killing him, and she really, really didn't want to be alone on the ocean at night.

Her father grasped her upper arms in his thick hands. He was a strong man and had probably been good-looking before a life of thieving, lying, and too much alcohol robbed him of his youth and his daughter's respect. "I'm dying."

Maddie's mouth opened, but no words came out.

"It's all right, love. The liver's gone. Cirrhosis. I'll be glad to be done with all of this." He gestured toward the door and the gunshots. "I'll miss seeing your mother ..." His eyes glossed over for a second before he focused in on her again. "And I'll miss you."

Maddie knew that was a lie. Though he took her mother on extravagant vacations several times a year, he rarely came to see Maddie, and this was the first time she'd been invited to go anywhere with him. It was turning out fabulous.

"But I've made my peace with God and man, and I'll die protecting my beautiful daughter."

Maddie had to bite her tongue, not sure how a pirate who fed off others' fears and misfortunes could make peace with anyone on heaven or earth. A banging on the door and a barrage of bullets into it announced Bello and his cronies. Maddie jumped but luckily didn't scream this time.

"The drive will explain everything, and it also has access to accounts that will make you a wealthy woman. Hold on to the papers if at all possible, but the drive is essential." He bent down and kissed her forehead then gave her a brief hug. "You're the best part of me, my love. Thank you for becoming so much better than I could've dreamed." He directed her into the boat and sat her down. It wasn't much bigger than a canoe, but it had a motor at the back. "When you get to land, follow the instructions. Someone I trust will come pick you up and help you create a new life and identity. Your mother too."

"But I just graduated." Six years of hard work down the crapper because of her father. If he wasn't dying, she'd be tempted to shoot him.

He smiled that placating smile parents gave to two-year-olds. "You can pick whatever degree you want. Don't go to Belize, Honduras, or Grand Cayman. Bello and the other pirate captains won't stop looking for you until the Coast Guard uses that information to capture them. America should be safe. They'll be more leery of the U.S. authorities." He nodded to her. "Be safe and be happy, my love."

Another barrage of bullets came at the door. Maddie's heart was in her throat. She had no clue how to say goodbye to a father who had caused her to doubt her worth her entire life. Yet she didn't want him to die from cirrhosis or Bello's gun. This was the first time in her life that he'd seemed to care, and now he would die protecting her from Bello.

Her father pushed a button, and before Maddie had time to say anything, the boat was lowered into the water. She clung to the sealed packet and the gun, watching her father's face.

"Start the motor," he yelled. "There's a pull cord at the back. Go." The ropes released her boat, and it almost capsized from the force of the yacht's wake. Maddie bit her lip to keep from crying out.

The compartment closed and the yacht sped off, her little boat bobbing in the waves. She held on to the side and prayed. Maddie could see men on deck with guns drawn. Luckily, it was a dark night and they didn't notice her. Soon the yacht was pinpricks of lights in the distance.

Maddie shuddered, set the packet and pistol underneath a seat, and turned to figure out how to start the motor. It wasn't cold, but her fingers felt like ice as she fumbled in the dark for switches and a pull cord. The boat reminded her of something she'd seen old men fishing in, a simple design with the motor and handle at the back that was used for steering.

"All the money in the world and this is his escape plan," she muttered. "If I built a secret compartment in a yacht, I would've put a James Bond boat in it, or something rocking cool. You're pathetic!" she yelled at her father. Too much distance and noise separated them for him to hear her. He'd never hear her again. A tear traced down her face, and she brushed it angrily away.

Tugging several times on the cord that would hopefully start the motor yielded nothing. She pulled out something she thought was a choke lever and yanked the pull cord again. The motor sounded but sputtered out after a few seconds. Maddie's cry of joy turned quickly to despair. She sat there for a few seconds, watching where the yacht had disappeared. When they discovered she was gone, would they come for her? Had they already ... killed her father? Another fat tear slid down her cheek, frustrating her. Ironic that all she'd wanted an hour ago was to disappear to any deserted island rather than spend another minute around her father and Bello. She should be more careful what she wished for.

She yanked on the motor cord again. It sprang to life but sputtered out. What was she forgetting? The choke thing had helped her start it, but was it just for starting?

Water splashed against the boat, and she could've sworn something smacked the side. She glanced around nervously, but it was too dark to see anything. Sharks? Eels? She had to get out of here.

Maddie's hands were slick with sweat as she pulled the starter one more time and then quickly pushed the choke lever forward. The motor stayed alive. *Yes!* She fumbled around with other levers until she must've put it into gear, because the boat sprang forward. Directing the rudder on the motor, she aimed away from where the yacht had gone and started praying. *Help me find land and someone nice who will help me.* She wasn't sure that she trusted anyone her father had arranged to get her to safety and set up a new identity. Why should she change her whole life because of her father or Bello? Maybe she could just appeal to Homeland Security, the FBI, or whatever governmental department dealt with pirates. They could catch Bello and the other pirate captains, and then she'd be safe. First, she needed to get through this huge ocean and find some help.

The wind started picking up, and Maddie's terror increased right along with it. The Caribbean was generally calmer than the Pacific or the Atlantic, but storms could come through and cover entire islands with waves. Her little boat wouldn't have a prayer in a real storm. *Please keep me safe. Please let the storm calm down.*

Her prayers didn't seem to be working. The wind whipped her hair out of its updo and tugged at the delicate lace overlay of her dress. Water splashed over the sides of the boat. She went up and down, wave after wave. The little boat barely stayed afloat, not seeming to make any progress.

She fumbled around with her left hand, but couldn't find a life jacket. Her dress clinging to her, Maddie shook from cold and wet as much as from fear. Everything around her was dark, and she wondered if she should have stayed on the yacht and taken her chances with Bello and his henchmen. No. Drowning was preferable to being in Bello's clutches without her father around to protect her. *Her father.* She could only imagine what Bello would do to him. What a horrible way to die.

A huge wave rocked her boat and soaked her clear through. Her heart clutched before picking up to staccato speed. She was going to die. This was it. She'd see her dad up in heaven a lot sooner than she'd planned. Well, maybe not. He definitely wasn't going to heaven, and she might've ruined her chances this past week when she'd regularly cursed all those men behind their backs. A valiant missionary she was not.

Maddie squinted through the darkness, searching, praying. She saw nothing. The water in the boat was up to her ankles. The little motor kept chugging along, but it seemed to be going slower. *Please, a little help*, she begged. She'd always communed with the good Lord, but never quite so frequently.

She wondered if she should stop and scoop water out of the boat, but then she'd have to release her hold on the lever directing her, and the boat might just spin in circles. She shoved heavy, wet hair from her face. Not that she knew what direction she was going in now. She instinctively reached for her cell phone, but it sat on her nightstand in the yacht. Since she didn't have an international plan, she'd stopped carrying it everywhere with her, but she could've at least used it as a compass.

Rain started pelting her from above as the waves splashed over her boat and hit her from below. "Really?" She tossed the words to the sky. "Hasn't my life been hard enough? Now I have to die in complete misery."

Truthfully, her life hadn't been too awful. Her mom was a professor at Montana State University, and they'd had a good life together in the small, beautiful mountain valley, loved and helped by friends and church members. Things only looked down when her father stole her mother away on some exotic vacation and left Maddie behind at her friend Abby's. Not that she didn't enjoy being with Abby, but she'd always dreamed of going with them on their trips. Now she'd finally gotten a taste of one of those vacations, and she couldn't believe her competent, smart mother had never divorced the louse.

Both her parents had lied to her throughout her life. "Papa's away on important business," her mother would always say. Ridiculous.

"Focus," Maddie muttered to herself. Blaming her parents wouldn't get her out of this predicament.

She scanned the darkness, praying, hoping. Blinking twice, she couldn't be sure if she'd really seen some lights, or if she was just getting delusional and desperate. But no ... or actually, yes. Yes! There were some dots of light to her left. She jerked the handle too hard in her excitement and almost capsized the boat. Yelping, she straightened it out and tried again more slowly.

A tingle of uncertainty lurked in her mind. What if it was the pirates coming back for her? But she really had no hope but to try for the lights. If it started to look like a ship, she'd change course. A full-size cruise ship would take her boat under, and a yacht had too much risk of being Bello.

As she slowly drew closer, she squinted to make out the shape of whatever she was approaching. The arrangement of lights looked too spread out to be a ship. It had to be an island. Letting out a squeal of joy, she leaned forward as if she could help the little boat go faster.

The island grew larger on the horizon. She could see lights down by the beach, and a cluster of windows were lit up on the hill. Details came into focus. It was one huge house—or maybe hotel—on the hill-top, and there was an inlet/harbor kind of thing. She could just make out the outline of a yacht in the harbor. There were some tiki torches on the beach a couple hundred yards away from the harbor and a fabulous long dock, stretching out into the ocean.

All she had to do was make it to the dock. She might crash into it due to her lack of boating skills, but she could grab the packet and swim for it if she had to. Hopefully, someone in that house or hotel would be trustworthy and willing to help. *Pathetic that she'd rather take her chances with strangers than trust her dad's people.* Not that her dad had ever put her in serious danger before.

Wait, that's all this trip had been: danger. Why had he brought her here now? Just to tell her he was dying, say goodbye, and have her clear his name? Couldn't he have done that without yucky Bello around?

Maddie saw movement on the long dock. A large man was waving his arms and yelling at her, but she couldn't make out his words.

The boat slammed into something. Maddie had no time to think or react as she flew over the front of the boat and plunged into the water.

***

I hope you enjoyed this excerpt from *Caribbean Rescue*. If you'd like to continue reading, click here.

EXCERPT FROM SHADOWS IN THE CURTAIN

by Cami Checketts

EMMALINE PRETENDED SHE DIDN'T FEEL his eyes on her as she strode to the leg press. It didn't matter where she was in the gym; he discreetly watched. She was flattered, but married. Although a beautiful distraction, she couldn't allow herself to be taken in by him.

She should've done one more set of rows, but she had to get out of there—get away from those blue eyes and back to the reality of the man she loved, the man she'd pledged her life to.

Emmy grabbed her keys and jacket from the shelves by the door and reached for the handle, mumbling a thank-you to the attendant. The door burst open from the outside; two teenagers scurried through. Emmy was knocked to the side and lost her balance. A pair of strong arms wrapped around her from behind, catching her. She found her footing, whirled in the man's embrace, and looked into pools of blue, sparkling like the ocean in Tahiti.

Her mouth hung open. Besides their exchange after *Joseph* several weeks ago, she'd kept her distance. She'd forced herself to forget those eyes with brown lashes longer than any woman's, the strong jawline and slightly hollowed cheeks that had dimples in them when he smiled —which he was doing right now.

"Are you okay, sweetheart?"

Her lips compressed. She was nobody's sweetheart but Grayson's. Emmy pulled free of his grasp. Risking one more glance into those eyes, she realized she needed to wipe the dimples from his face before she tripped on purpose so he'd catch her again. "Tell me you have a beautiful wife and at least two adorable children at home and you're just smiling at me because you're an incredibly nice guy who has no agenda where I'm concerned."

Dimples erased. He exhaled slowly, eyes darkening like a storm blowing in. "No wife and no adorable children."

Emmy folded her arms across her chest. To his credit, his eyes didn't rove from hers, but when she thought about it, they never did. Every time she caught his gaze on her, he was looking at her face, not her body.

"Yeah, well, I do," she said. "Awesome husband, that is, and he wouldn't appreciate the way you're always checking me out."

He didn't look away, nor did he deny it. He brushed a hand through his longish sandy-blond hair before nodding slowly. "You're right. I, um, never noticed a ring or had the guts to talk to you before now. Now that I know you're married ..." He swallowed. "... I won't bother you again."

Something inside her melted at the sad look in his eyes and his admission that he hadn't dared approach her and wouldn't have even been looking if she'd worn her ring. It was just obnoxiously huge and rubbed against her finger when she lifted weights. She'd buy a gold band today.

"Thanks." For some reason, she wanted to reassure him, maybe bring back one of the dimples. She forced a smile. "No worries for you, since every other woman in Cannon Beach is after you." Did that sound as awkward to him as it did to her?

He frowned and held the door open for her. She nodded to him before slinking through the door and could've sworn he said, "But not the right woman."

Waves softly crashed on the beach a hundred feet from their home. Emmy leaned on the deck railing, soaking up the new day, the salt in the air, her wet hair dampening her shirt, and the sun warming her forehead. She only had fifteen minutes to dry her dark hair, put some makeup on, and eat breakfast before her first voice student showed up, but she wanted to sit and watch the ocean, go on a walk, or better yet, take a long swim.

Grayson came up behind her, resting his chin on top of her head. She smiled at the feel of his tall, gangly body wrapped around her. He was so comfortable to lean against. They'd spent their teenage years as neighbors and best friends. Grayson had pursued her for years before she agreed to marry him. Then he'd moved her away from the craziness of L.A. and the theater crowd who would trample anyone to be on top. Now she acted at a lesser theater with people she adored, taught music to sweet children, and loved every minute with her husband. With the exception of the disturbing notes, the past year had been the most content and peaceful time of her life.

"You want to go swimming?" he guessed.

She sighed. "Yes, but I've got a student coming any minute and I'm sure you have a lot of work to do."

He kissed her hair. "I'll watch you when I get home." He'd opened a branch of his software company in Portland and enjoyed driving into work on occasion, but he ended up flying to his main facility in L.A. at least twice a week. He was gone more than she liked, but he took his success and his products very seriously.

"Thanks," she said. "That would be great."

Grayson assumed she would give up swimming in the ocean when they'd moved to the cooler waters of Oregon. She argued that with a full-length wetsuit, she was as warm as she'd been in California. He'd finally played the petrified husband card and made her swear to only swim if he came with her or watched from the beach. She didn't doubt his love, but sometimes she felt smothered. Her acting career was just like her swimming. He had come to every practice and performance he could since the threatening notes began. If he realized men were hitting on her at the gym, he'd get a membership tomorrow.

He pressed a soft kiss to her lips. As always, Emmy hoped for passion to ignite within her at his kiss. As always, it was pleasant and short.

She glanced back at the beach and saw the man from the gym. Swallowing, she forced herself not to react. *What is he doing here?* He met her gaze.

She drew a couple of shaky breaths before turning and focusing on her husband.

The ringing phone gave her an excuse to go inside.

"Drive safe," Emmy said to Grayson as she walked into their two-story living room and reached for the cordless on the coffee table.

"Love you." Grayson closed the sliding glass door and then left through the garage entrance off the laundry room.

"Love you too." She pushed the button on the phone. "Hello."

"Emmaline," Aunt Jalina's voice screeched in her ear. "I read some wonderful reviews about your performance in *Joseph*. I'd be proud if you were actually performing with a company worth being called a company."

"Good morning, Auntie." Emmy shook her head. Aunt Jalina sounded in good spirits.

"It's an awful morning. When are you going to come home, or at least make that skinny husband of yours move you to Portland so you can perform with a respectable group?"

"And give up this view?" Emmy paused and smiled at the truth of her statement. Two-story windows showcased waves crashing on the beach. Haystack Rock decorated the background. "Not a chance. How's Uncle Carl?"

"Happy as ever—sends you his love."

Emmy smiled. At least she knew that her uncle loved her. Her aunt did in her own twisted way, but sometimes it was hard to feel through the criticism. "Give him a kiss for me. I've got to run; students are on their way."

"Students? You waste your abilities teaching children who could never rise to the talent and training you've been blessed with."

Emmy walked into the kitchen and put some bread in the toaster. "Oh, I don't know about that. I've got some very promising children here."

"Pshaw. You may think it's fun to tease me, Emmaline, but your mother would be rolling over in her grave."

Emmy clutched the butter knife in her hand. "Now that's where you're wrong, Auntie. My mother was proud of me no matter what."

"Your mother was proud because you were a success! What are you now? A twenty-five-year-old who's already washed up and given up."

Emmy stood to her full five feet six inches. She knew all her mother would've wanted was her happiness. "I am successful at what I'm doing. I'm happy and respected here. I'd never go back to that cesspool of cutthroats."

Jalina clucked her tongue. "Darling, I know you didn't enjoy L.A. I'm not saying you have to move back here, but please consider auditioning in Portland at least."

"Did I not speak clearly? I am happy here."

"Don't you get uppity with me! If you don't do something with your life ..." She paused, then continued with her shrill voice. "I will cut you out of my inheritance."

Emmy laughed at that. Jalina had no clue how wealthy Grayson was and how little Emmy cared for the money. "Oh, Auntie, when has money ever been a motivator for me?"

"It should be! You know how horrible it is to go without."

Emmy's young life had been filled with want as her mother earned just enough to survive. Somehow there had always been money for Emmy's acting, vocal, and piano lessons. She'd been too young and loved the lessons too much to question why they didn't have enough food but could afford the best private tutors. "Don't pretend you don't feel guilty about that," Emmy said.

"If your mother wouldn't have lied to us all those years. She would only let me pay for your lessons. I had no clue."

She didn't go on, and Emmy was grateful. Her aunt and uncle were devastated when they'd finally forced her mother to let them visit her dilapidated Detroit apartment. They saw for themselves that Emmy's mother could barely afford rent and food, living off a waitress's salary after Emmy's father deserted them. Uncle Carl and Aunt Jalina moved them to Glendora, California, and spoiled them both until her mother died three years ago from the cancer that ate away her breasts and then her vital organs. Even though she'd been twenty-one, Emmy hadn't been prepared to lose her mom. She missed her mother's quiet and unfailing love.

Her aunt insisted Emmy finish her M.F.A. from American Conservatory Theater in San Francisco before auditioning with the best companies in L.A. At twenty-four she had been an acclaimed performer, but miserable. She had no hope of rescue until Grayson talked her into marrying him and moved her away from it all.

A loud rap came from the sliding glass door.

"I've got a student here, Auntie." Emmy hung up without waiting for goodbye and motioned to her next-door neighbor to come in. "Student" was a loose term to use—she considered Kelton and his family her closest friends.

Kelton's white teeth split his copper skin as he thrust the back door open. "How's the prettiest voice teacher in Cannon Beach?"

"*Only* voice teacher in Cannon Beach." Emmy rolled her eyes. "I'll be better when I hear you practiced every day this week."

"Ha. We both know I only take lessons so I can come visit you and keep my momma from kicking me in the butt." The brawny defender for Seaside High's lacrosse team made it clear that hitting the gym and flirting with girls were more important than developing his musical ability.

Emmy shook her head, hiding a smile at his usual antics. The boy was inappropriate, but she loved him like the nephew she'd never had. "We're both going to kick your behind if you don't start practicing."

Kelton shrugged innocently and made his way to the piano. Emmy forgot about missing breakfast, her aunt, and the man from the gym as she played the piano and encouraged her uncommitted yet talented neighbor.

***

I hope you enjoyed this excerpt from *Shadows in the Curtain*. To continue reading click here.

ALSO BY CAMI CHECKETTS

Rescued by Love: Park City Firefighter Romance

Reluctant Rescue: Park City Firefighter Romance

The Resilient One: Billionaire Bride Pact Romance

The Feisty One: Billionaire Bride Pact Romance

The Independent One: Billionaire Bride Pact Romance

The Protective One: Billionaire Bride Pact Romance

The Faithful One: Billionaire Bride Pact Romance

The Daring One: Billionaire Bride Pact Romance

Pass Interference: A Last Play Romance

How to Love a Dog's Best Friend

Oh, Come On, Be Faithful

Shadows in the Curtain: Billionaire Beach Romance

Caribbean Rescue: Billionaire Beach Romance

Cozumel Escape: Billionaire Beach Romance

Cancun Getaway: Billionaire Beach Romance

Protect This

Blog This

Redeem This

The Broken Path

Dead Running

Dying to Run

Running Home

Full Court Devotion: Christmas in Snow Valley

A Touch of Love: Summer in Snow Valley

Running from the Cowboy: Spring in Snow Valley

Made in the USA
Columbia, SC
30 March 2019